TRADING PLACES
with TANK TALBOTT

Dori Hillestad Butler

Albert Whitman & Company
Morton Grove, Illinois

For Bob, because this one is special.

Library of Congress Cataloging-in-Publication Data

Butler, Dori Hillestad.
Trading places with Tank Talbott / by Dori Hillestad Butler.
p. cm.
Summary: Jason, who would rather work on his horror movie screenplay
than learn to swim, finds an unlikely ally in Tank, the class bully,
who is being forced to take ballroom dance lessons.
ISBN 0-8075-1708-9 (hardcover)
ISBN 0-8075-8060-0 (paperback)
[1. Swimming—Fiction. 2. Dance—Fiction. 3. Authorship—Fiction.
4. Friendship—Fiction. 5. Bullies—Fiction.] I. Title.
PZ7.B9759 Tr 2003 [Fic]—dc21 2002012383

Cover art by Barry Gott.
The typeface is New Century Schoolbook.
The design is by Mary-Ann Lupa.

For more information about Albert Whitman & Company,
visit our web site at www.albertwhitman.com.

Table of Contents

1
Swimming Test

Jason Pfeiffer rested his chin against the car door and stared out the open window as the world went by. He tried not to think about where he was going.

Good thoughts, he reminded himself. Think good thoughts. Like *The Dagmartian*. That was a good thought. *The Dagmartian* was the movie he was writing about a two-headed beast that bubbled up from the bottom of a swimming pool and attacked people. It was such a cool idea. One day *The Dagmartian* would earn him an Academy Award for Best Script or Best Director. Maybe even both.

Jason could see it now. His name in lights. People begging for his autograph. Reporters wanting to know how he got the idea for such a scary creature...

"Hey," Jason's sister, Dagmar, poked his arm. "Roll up your window. The wind's messing up my hair." She flipped her mane of dark brown hair over her shoulder.

Jason gasped at the creature who shared the back seat with him. It was the Dagmartian. In the flesh!

If he rolled up his window, he'd be trapped. The Dagmartian would wrap her tentacles around him and suck the life right out of him.

There was only one thing to do. Jason pulled up his legs, leaned as far into his corner of the car as he could, and screamed bloody murder.

Mom slammed on the brakes and the car screeched to a halt. "What? What's the matter?"

"Nothing," Jason said. "I thought I saw a creature from another planet, but it's okay. It's just Dagmar."

Dagmar rolled her eyes. "All I want is for him to put up his window. Is that so much to ask?"

The car started moving again and Mom glared at Jason in the rearview mirror. "You're eleven years old, Jason. You should know better than to scream when I'm driving."

"Sorry," Jason said, pushing up his glasses.

"Roll up the window," Mom ordered. "And no fighting back there!"

Dagmar put on this look like "Who me? Fight with him?" Yeah, right. From the day Jason was born, Dagmar had done nothing but torture him. She hated him. She told him so all the time.

She pinched him, scratched him, pinned him against a wall until he promised to do whatever disgusting chore she was trying to get out of.

She was three years older than he was. And a whole head taller. Jason was no match for her. His only defense was to put her in his horror movies. He could hardly wait to see his sister's face at the opening of *The Dagmartian*. Revenge for all those years of abuse.

"Here we are," Mom said cheerfully as she pulled into the driveway in front of the Rec Center. "Are you ready, Jason?"

Jason's heart pounded. The only thing worse than sharing breathing space with his sister was having to go to his swimming lesson. Especially on test day.

"I don't feel so good," Jason moaned.

"Oh, Jason," Mom said. "You always say that."

"But I really don't," Jason insisted. His stomach felt like it had grown a million feet. And all those feet were running and jumping and kicking inside him.

Mom reached over from the front seat and felt his forehead. "I think you're just nervous."

No lie, Jason thought. Every time he went near the pool, he remembered what happened at Grandpa Larson's cabin last August. It was April now, but the memory was just as strong.

Grandpa had taken Jason and Dagmar out fishing on the lake. Jason wasn't sure what happened. Just that one minute he was in the boat, the next he was in the water. Without his life jacket. It all happened so fast.

Water had washed over his head and rushed into his nose and mouth. It tasted like dead fish and rotting weeds. Jason gagged. He tried to cough, but he couldn't. Couldn't get rid of the water.

3

Desperately, he clawed at the water, struggling to get to the surface. He had to breathe. Had to get air. But he couldn't. He was going down. Down to the bottom of the lake.

It was true what they said about your whole life passing before your eyes when you die.

Except Jason didn't die.

Eventually, Grandpa got his big arm around Jason's middle and fished him out of the water. Then he pounded on Jason's back until Jason threw up all the lake water that he'd swallowed.

When Mom heard what happened, she said, "That's it! You need to learn to swim."

Jason had never taken swimming lessons. He never wanted to. Swimming was Dagmar's thing, not his. Jason preferred writing and acting.

But now Jason had no choice. If he ever wanted more writing or acting classes, he would have to pass tadpole swimming first.

"I know you can do this, Jason," Mom said gently as she waited for him to get out of the car. "I know you can put your fears aside and learn to swim."

Why did grownups always think they knew you could do something when really you couldn't? Like last fall when that jerk Tank Talbott broke Jason's best friend Luke Murphy's nose. Their teacher, Mr. Burns, had actually said, "I know you boys can put

4

your differences aside and learn to get along."

Right. Tank had been hassling Luke since the day his family moved in next door to Luke's. Half the time Luke couldn't even play outside in his own backyard because Tank would come over and beat him up. How was Luke supposed to just "put aside" six years of that? What finally happened was Luke moved to Texas during Christmas vacation.

Too bad Jason couldn't move away from swimming lessons.

"Go on, now." Mom nodded at the door. "I need to go park the car. I'll see you inside."

Jason forced himself to open the door and get out.

"Remember!" Mom stuck her head out her window. "Positive attitude! If you think you can do it, you can."

Right, Jason thought as he trudged up the zillion and one steps that led to the Rec Center. He opened the heavy glass door and headed left toward the pool area. A chlorine smell hung in the air.

Jason's swimming teacher, Mr. Abram, was reading a magazine at the front desk.

"Hello, Jason." Mr. Abram said. He didn't even look up from his magazine.

Jason knew that Mr. Abram only liked kids who got right in the pool, put their faces in the water, and did what they were told to do.

Jason took his glasses off. He was about to leave

them at the desk like he always did when suddenly he got an idea.

He cleared his throat to get Mr. Abram's attention. "Um, if you want, you could just give me my green slip now. Go ahead and mark *fail* on it."

Mr. Abram looked up at Jason. "Don't you at least want to take the test first?"

Jason shrugged. "I've taken it two times already." And failed it both times.

Mr. Abram scratched his head. "This test is very simple. All you have to do is tread water for two minutes, float on your back, and swim the crawl one length of the pool."

Yeah. Real simple. "Do I have to put my face in the water for the crawl?" Jason asked.

"It wouldn't be a crawl stroke if you didn't."

"Then I'll take my green slip now," Jason repeated. There was no point in even getting in the water.

Mr. Abram sighed. "Have it your way." He picked up a tablet of green test forms, wrote Jason's name on the first one and circled the word *fail*. He tore the top paper off and handed it to Jason. "Here you go," he said.

"Thanks." Jason put his glasses back on. He felt like a huge weight had been lifted from his shoulders. He ran back outside and met his mom and sister coming up the steps.

Jason handed his mother the green slip.

Dagmar peered at the slip over Mom's shoulder. "You flunked?" she asked. "How could you flunk already? All we did was park the car."

"I told Mr. Abram he didn't have to give me the test." Jason explained. "I knew I'd fail."

"How can you know you're going to fail before you ever even take the test?" Mom asked.

Jason raised an eyebrow. Some things were obvious, weren't they?

"All right," Mom said. "Let's go in and find out when the next session starts." She turned to Dagmar. "Maybe you want to go back to swim team again next session, too? You've had several months off."

"No!" Dagmar cried. "I already told you, I'm not just taking a break here. I don't want to do swim team anymore! I don't want to do swim team ever again!"

"But you love swim team," Mom said. Dagmar had been on the swim team for as long as Jason could remember. Her bedroom overflowed with swimming ribbons, medals, and trophies.

"I *used* to love it," Dagmar corrected.

"Okay, okay," Mom said. Sometimes, there was no reasoning with Dagmar. "Come on, Jason."

Jason shuffled along behind her. "How come she can quit swimming and I can't?"

"Quitting swim team and quitting swimming lessons are two different things," Mom said.

7

"Yeah, but it's still not fair. If I promise to stay away from water my whole life, do I still have to take more lessons?"

"You're *never* going to go near water?" Mom looked doubtful.

"Never," Jason promised, crossing his heart.

"Never go in a boat?"

"Definitely not!" Not after last summer.

"Never film one of your movies near water?"

Jason thought about *The Dagmartian*. "Well, I won't have to get in the water for that," he said. "My movie director's chair will sort of swivel out over the water."

"What if you fall off your chair?" Dagmar asked.

"I won't."

"I'm sorry, Jason," Mom shook her head. "But you know the deal. Learning how to swim is a matter of life and death. Once you learn enough to pass tadpole swimming, you can quit. But until then, you have to keep taking lessons."

Jason's shoulders slumped. He was going to be taking tadpole swimming lessons for the rest of his life.

2
Dork Face

Hey, Dork Face!" A mean voice startled Jason when he walked up the Rec Center steps on Thursday afternoon.

Jason turned. Oh, no. What was Tank Talbott doing here?

Tank didn't know it, but he had a small role in Jason's movie, too. He was the Turbo-Tank, a twelve-foot-tall monster with a head like an army tank and a body like a human's. The Turbo-Tank came charging out of the woods in Scene 2, but the Dagmartian ripped him apart with her razor-sharp claws and ate him for a midnight snack. It was an awesome scene. Or it would be once it was on the big screen. Blood and machine parts would be flying everywhere.

"What are you doing here, Dork Face?" Tank asked as he fell into step beside Jason. "Taking *dance* lessons?"

"No!" Jason replied, his voice cracking.

Jason was the same height as Tank. He had the same build, too. It was possible he could hold his own against Tank. Possible, but not very likely. As far as Jason knew, his only interest was beating people up.

Jason continued up the steps. "I'm just, you know, here to hang out." He hoped he sounded relaxed. Jason figured the best way to deal with a guy like Tank was to pretend you weren't afraid of him.

"Yeah, that's what I'm doing here, too," Tank said. He yanked open the door. "I'm hanging out."

Jason swallowed hard. He hoped Tank wasn't going to *hang out* at the pool!

When they got inside, Jason saw the sign. *Ballroom Dance for Kids.* An arrow pointed toward the gym.

Jason and Tank both stopped.

"Well?" Tank said, hands on his hips. "Which way are you going, Dork Face?"

Jason started toward the pool. But he glanced back over his shoulder. Tank was still staring at him.

"Don't even think it!" Tank jabbed a finger at Jason. His eyes narrowed into angry little slits. "I'm here to play basketball, not take dance lessons!"

Jason held up his hands in innocence. "Sure, Tank. Whatever you say." The truth was, Jason didn't care what Tank was doing here. As long as he wasn't taking tadpole swimming class.

* * *

Jason stood shivering at the edge of the pool with the other tadpole swimmers. Was it his imagination, or were the other kids who took tadpole swimming getting shorter? Jason towered over everyone this time.

"I'm Ms. Hall," said a woman who was wearing a dark red one-piece Rec Center swimming suit. Her brown hair bounced on her shoulders as she walked back and forth in front of the group. "I'm going to be your swimming teacher."

Cool, Jason thought. A new teacher. Not like a new teacher was any more likely to get him to swim than Mr. Abram was. But it was still nice to have a fresh start.

"You can't learn to swim by standing around." Ms. Hall blew on her whistle. "Everybody in the pool!"

"Hooray!" several kids shouted.

All around Jason, kids dive-bombed into the pool. Jason stepped back so he wouldn't be splashed. He couldn't help it. Every time he looked into the water, he saw a shapeless monster that wanted to swallow him up and drag him to that dark place at the bottom of the pool where he wouldn't be able to see or hear or breathe.

"I said *everybody* in the pool," Ms. Hall repeated with a pointed look at Jason.

Jason slowly sat down at the edge of the pool and lowered himself into the water.

Brr! Goosebumps ran up his arms.

"How many of you know how to blow bubbles?" Ms. Hall asked once everyone was lined up.

Jason glanced down the line. Even without his glasses, he could see that everyone else raised a hand, so he slowly raised his hand, too. Besides, he knew how to blow bubbles. He just couldn't do it.

When everyone else put their faces in the water, Jason touched his chin to the water. When everyone else ducked down under the water, Jason went down as far as his shoulders.

He glanced down the line of tadpole swimmers again. Usually there were one or two other kids like him. Kids who couldn't put their faces in the water. But this time every head but his was wet. This wasn't good.

Keeping both feet planted firmly on the pool floor, Jason crouched down, squeezed his eyes shut, plugged his nose and dipped the back of his head into the water. When he stood back up, water ran down his shoulders. There. His head was wet.

Ms. Hall blew her whistle. "We have ten minutes left. I want you all to do five jellyfish, five starfish, and five torpedoes."

Ms. Hall started down the line of swimmers. Jason tried to hide behind the kid next to him, but it was hard to hide behind someone who was shorter than he was.

Ms. Hall stopped in front of Jason. "I haven't seen your face go in the water."

"Really?" Jason let out a nervous laugh. "Gee, I don't know how you could've missed it." He scratched his head, hoping she'd notice how wet it was.

"What's your name?" Ms. Hall asked.

"Jason."

"Well, Jason, let's see your jellyfish."

Jason's heart thumped. A jellyfish was when you put your face in the water and held your legs up under you.

Jason couldn't do a jellyfish. But Ms. Hall was waiting, so he had to do something. He took a deep breath, pinched his nose shut, and stuck his face in the water for about half a second.

"There," he said as water dripped from his face. He rubbed his eyes. "How was that?"

"It's a start." Ms. Hall smiled. "By the end of the session, we'll have you putting your face in the water *without* plugging your nose."

Dream on, Jason thought.

When it was time to leave, Jason was the first one out of the pool. He ran to the boys' locker room and got dressed in record time. Then he headed out to the lobby to pick up his glasses and wait for his mom to pick him up.

"Hey, Jason!" Ms. Hall called from the desk. "You forgot your glasses!"

Jason squinted. Ms. Hall wasn't talking to him. She was talking to Tank Talbott.

Wow, Jason had never realized how much he and

Tank looked sort of alike from the back.

Tank swung his gym bag back and forth next to the door.

Ms. Hall came around the desk and brought Jason's glasses over to Tank.

No! Jason hurried across the lobby. Knowing Tank, he'd probably toss the glasses on the floor and stomp on them.

But all Tank did was look at the glasses like they were some kind of fungus. "Those aren't mine," he said. "They're *his*." Tank pointed at Jason.

Ms. Hall turned. "Oh!" she said with surprise. She looked from Jason to Tank and back at Jason. "Well, you two look so much alike."

"No, we don't!" Tank curled his upper lip in disgust.

"Well, not up close," Ms. Hall agreed. "I'm sorry for the confusion. Here are your glasses, Jason."

"Thanks," Jason said, putting them on.

Tank raised his eyes to the ceiling. "Could my day possibly get any worse?" he asked. "Someone actually thought I was Jason Pfeiffer."

Before Jason could respond, a short, grandmotherly lady came from the gym. She wore a blue sweater that somehow sort of matched her hair. She looked at the boys and smiled. "We had some problems today, Tank," she said, her smile fading just a little. "But next time will be better."

Jason was surprised that a lady that old was teaching basketball.

"Remember what I said about that side step. Use the inside of your foot to make a smooth transition from one foot to another."

Smooth transition? Jason looked at Tank.

"Side-together, side-together, side-together," the lady said as she sidestepped a semicircle around them.

Tank's face turned red.

Jason scratched his chin. This was the most interesting "basketball" move he'd ever seen.

3

Please Don't Rearrange My Face

Tank grabbed Jason by the shirt and shoved him against the wall. "What are you grinning at, Dork Face?"

Jason looked around the lobby. Ms. Hall and the grandmotherly lady had left. He was alone with Tank.

"I said, what are you grinning at?" Tank repeated.

"I-I-I'm not grinning at anything," Jason stammered. What, now that Luke was gone, was Tank going to make Jason his new punching bag?

Tank narrowed his eyes. "If you tell anyone I'm taking dance lessons, you're dead meat! Understand?" Tank got right in Jason's face. Jason could smell the tuna fish sandwich Tank must have eaten for lunch. "UNDERSTAND?"

"S-s-sure, Tank. Whatever you say." At least if Tank decided to kill him, he wouldn't have to take swimming lessons anymore.

Tank glowered at Jason. He let Jason go, then stomped to the door. "Where's my mom?" he muttered, staring out through the glass.

Jason was wondering the same thing about *his* mom. But he didn't want to stand next to Tank. He sat down on the bench to wait. Tank sighed heavily and plopped down beside Jason.

Jason cleared his throat. "Dance lessons aren't so bad," he said, trying to be helpful.

Tank glared at him.

"I'm only taking these lessons because my mom's making me," Tank said. "My sister's wedding is coming up, and my mom thinks we're all going to dance."

"Too bad," Jason said. He didn't know what else to say.

"At least there aren't any kids I know there," Tank went on. "The only one who knows I'm taking this stupid class is you. And you don't really count."

Jason took that as a good sign. He didn't count. He wasn't worth Tank's time. Wasn't worth beating up.

Tank gazed out over the parking lot. "Man, I'd do anything to get out of these lessons," he said, slumping back against the wall.

Jason knew exactly how Tank felt.

As long as Tank was being honest, Jason said, "I'd do anything to get out of my swimming lessons, too."

Tank looked at Jason. "Swimming lessons are nothing like dancing lessons."

"They are if you don't like to put your face in the water." As soon as the words were out of Jason's mouth, he wished he could suck them back in.

"You can't put your face in the water?" Tank laughed.

"You're even more of a doofus than I thought you were."

"What about you?" Jason asked. He stood up. "What's so hard about step-together, step-together?" Jason copied the grandmotherly lady's moves.

Tank stood up. His nostrils flared.

Uh-oh, Jason thought. Tank was going to pound him for sure now.

"Are you saying I'm *stupid*?" Tank took a step toward Jason.

"N-n-no," Jason took a step back. "Of course not. And I don't think dancing is stupid, either. I-I-I just think s-s-swimming is stupid."

Tank had that look in his eye. The Turbo-Tank look. The look that said *you're going to get it now!*

Jason had to think of something. Fast.

He was closer to the door than Tank was. He could make a run for it. He could toss his swimming bag at Tank to distract him and then he could run!

But then he got another idea. A *good* idea.

Tank frowned. "*Now* what are you grinning at?"

Jason couldn't help grinning. This was it! Not only the answer to his prayers, but the answer to Tank's, too. And maybe, if Jason could do something to help Tank, maybe Tank would leave him alone?

Jason took a deep breath. "What if you and I trade places?"

"Trade places?" Tank leered at Jason.

"You take my swimming lessons for me..."

"No way!" Tank shook his head.

"Shhh!" Jason glanced toward the pool area. He didn't want anyone but Tank to hear this. "Just listen! You take my swimming lessons for me. And then I'll take your dancing lessons for you."

Tank blinked. "You'd take my dancing lessons for me?"

"Yup."

"*All* of them?" Tank's brown eyes widened.

"If you take all of my swimming lessons. Including the test at the end. And you *pass*."

Yes! This was his way out of swimming lessons!

"Tadpole swimming lessons, right? With the little kids?" Tank wasn't laughing at him this time. He actually seemed to be thinking about it.

"I don't know anybody in the class," Jason said in a rush. "I've even got a different teacher this time. No one will know."

Tank was still thinking.

"Think about how much you hate dance lessons," Jason said. "I mean, for a guy like me, they're fine. But a guy like you? Totally uncool!"

Tank narrowed his eyes. "You think *tadpole* swimming lessons are cool?"

"Well, no, but—"

"We probably could get away with it," Tank said thoughtfully. He sat back down.

"Sure we could," Jason agreed. He sat down beside Tank. "You and I look a lot alike."

"Don't remind me."

"But we do!" Jason insisted. "My swimming teacher couldn't tell the difference."

Tank drummed his fingers against his chin. "Okay. Meet me in the main bathroom before lessons on Thursday," Tank said. "We'll swap clothes and stuff in there."

"Okay!" Jason cried. He could hardly keep the excitement out of his voice.

"And mellow out, would you?" Tank said. "You're spitting on me." He brushed some imaginary spit off his arm.

When Jason's mom finally showed up, he ran out the door to the parking lot.

"I'm sorry I'm late," Mom said when Jason got to the car. "I got stuck at a railroad crossing. How did your swimming lesson go?"

"Pretty good." Jason couldn't stop the grin from spreading across his face. "Better than usual!"

Mom glanced at him over her shoulder. "Really?"

"Oh yeah." Jason nodded. After all, this was the last time he would ever have to take tadpole swimming lessons. He would never have to set foot in a pool again.

The weird thing was he owed it all to Tank Talbott.

That night, Jason instant messaged Luke. Ever since Luke moved away, they used the computer to stay in touch.

Moviemaker: You'll never believe what happened today.
Cool_Luke324: What?
Moviemaker: I ran into Tank Talbott at the Rec Center. He's taking dance lessons.
Cool_Luke324: Tank Talbott in a dance class? HAHAHAHAHAHAHA!
Moviemaker: Wait! There's more! Tank hates dancing. And I hate swimming. So… we're going to trade places. Tank's going to take my swimming lessons and I'm going to take his dance lessons.

It took Luke a long time to write back. A really long time.

Moviemaker: Are u still there?
Cool_Luke324: You made a deal with TANK?
Moviemaker: Why not? We're the same height. We have the same color hair. The lady at the Rec Center even thought Tank was me.
Cool_Luke324: That's a really bad idea!
Moviemaker: Why? I know he's a jerk. But I can help him and he can help me. We both win.

Cool_Luke324: Nobody ever wins with Tank.
U can't trust him. He probably won't even show up.
And if he does, he'll probably just get U in trouble.

Jason hadn't thought of that. What if Tank didn't show up? Or what if he did show up and started beating up the little kids in the pool? But Jason couldn't worry about that now.

Moviemaker: Look, I'm never going to learn to swim, okay? And if I can't get out of those swimming lessons soon, I'm gonna...
Cool_Luke324: Gonna what?
Moviemaker: I don't know. But it won't be good.
Cool_Luke324: Well, be careful.
Moviemaker: I will.
Cool_Luke324: Because Tank's not like you. At all.

Luke was right, Jason thought. Still, Tank Talbott was the only chance he had.

4
Trading Places

Y ou've got to be kidding!" Tank stared at the
swimsuit in Jason's hand. "You expect me to
wear that?"

Jason looked at his swimsuit. "What's wrong
with it?"

"It's got *ducks* on it. Geez, Pfeiffer! Do you go out
of your way to be a geek, or what?"

"No!" Jason replied. He just hadn't gotten a new
swimsuit in a while. He pushed his glasses up on his
nose. "It's the only one I have," he said.

Tank shook his head. "You are such a dork." He
snatched the swimsuit out of Jason's hand, then went
into one of the toilet stalls to get changed.

"I feel like I'm in that movie *Invasion of the Body
Snatchers*," Tank muttered.

Jason paced back and forth in front of the stall.
His heart hammered in his chest. They were really
going to do this. They were going to trade places.

Would people believe he was Tank Talbott?

Would people believe Tank Talbott was him? A lot
depended on how Tank acted.

Jason cleared his throat. "Remember, your name is

Jason Pfeiffer, not Tank Talbott."

Tank snorted as he came out of the bathroom stall. "As long as I'm wearing this suit, I'm not going to forget," he said, tossing his school clothes in a pile in the corner. Jason stared at Tank. It felt strange to see Tank Talbott wearing *his* swimsuit. He had to admit, the ducks *did* look a little stupid.

Jason cleared his throat again. "Just don't swim around like you've been doing it your whole life."

"I *have* been doing it my whole life."

"Well, pretend you haven't!" Jason said. "I think you're going to learn the dead-man's float today."

"Big whoop."

"Remember, you can't do it! Don't put your face in the water. Not until the very end. Then do it really slowly. Like it's the first time you've ever done it."

"Yeah, yeah."

Jason bit his lip. Tank didn't seem to be taking this very seriously. "Maybe you should practice."

Tank grabbed Jason's towel. "Practice what?"

Jason swallowed hard. "Practice acting, well, *scared*," he said in a small voice. He couldn't imagine Tank Talbott ever feeling scared about anything.

"I think I know how to act like a dork, Dork Face. The question is, do you know how to act like a normal person?"

"Oh, yeah. I've taken acting classes," Jason said,

trying to be funny.

Tank snorted. "I'm sure."

"So...is there anything I should know about your dance class?" Jason asked, following Tank to the door.

Tank chewed his lip thoughtfully. "Not really."

"Well, okay then." Jason took his glasses off and handed them to Tank. "I leave my glasses with the person who's working at the desk," he said.

"Okay." Tank slipped the glasses into the back pocket of Jason's swimsuit.

"No! You have to *wear* them to the desk," Jason insisted. "I always wear my glasses."

Tank sighed. He put the glasses on. "I can't see with these things," he complained.

Didn't Tank get how important it was that they each act exactly like the other? Otherwise someone would figure out what they were up to.

"Well, I can't see without them," Jason said. "I'm going to have to go through your whole dance lesson without being able to see anything."

"Lucky you," Tank said. He leaned close and hissed in Jason's ear. "The girls in there are really ugly!"

* * *

The Rec Center gym smelled like dirty socks. But Jason would rather smell dirty socks than chlorine any day. Even without his glasses, Jason could see that he wasn't the tallest kid in this class. In fact, he was one of the shortest. This was supposed to be a ballroom dance class for *kids*, but some of these girls were so tall they were practically *women!* Which brought Jason to his next question — where were the other boys?

A couple of the girl/women people looked at Jason and he held his breath, waiting to see if someone would point a finger at him and say, "You fake! You're not Tank Talbott!"

But no one did. The girls headed right to the grand-motherly lady. Today she was wearing a green sweater instead of a blue one.

What if she remembers me? Jason worried.

"We have something for you, Mrs. Kaplan," one of the girls said.

"It's a protest," said a girl who had a long red braid.

"No, it's a petition," another girl corrected. She turned to Mrs. Kaplan. "My dad says that if there's something you and a bunch of other people don't want to do, you should write it down on a piece of paper and have everyone sign it."

"So that's what we did," said a third girl. She handed Mrs. Kaplan a sheet of paper.

"I see," Mrs. Kaplan said slowly. "And what is it you don't want to do?" She picked up the glasses that she wore on a chain around her neck and put them on. Then she read the paper out loud. "We the undersigned hereby refuse to dance with Tank Talbott now and forever."

Jason grinned. Boy, that Tank made enemies everywhere he went, didn't he?

But Jason's smile froze when everyone turned to glare at him. He'd forgotten that for the moment, he *was* Tank.

"I don't know what to say," Mrs. Kaplan said, running her hand through her curls. "Tank is our only boy. I'm really surprised that *no one* wants to dance with him."

Jason's jaw dropped. Tank never said anything about him being the *only* boy.

"He stomps on our feet," one girl complained.

"And he pulls hair." Another girl rubbed her scalp.

"Sometimes he even makes rude comments!" A third girl folded her arms across her chest and narrowed her eyes at Jason.

Tank did all that? People thought *he* did all that?

Jason took a step back. Two minutes ago he was afraid no one would think he was really Tank.

Now he was afraid everyone would think he *was*.

"We did have some problems last time, Tank," Mrs. Kaplan said, her hands on her hips. "But I didn't know they were this serious. What do you have to say for yourself?"

"Uh..." Jason didn't know what to say. "I'm sorry?" he tried.

"As well you should be," Mrs. Kaplan pursed her lips. "Well, I can certainly understand why no one wants to be your partner, Tank. So as long as everyone's here and we have an odd number, I won't force anyone to dance with you."

"Hooray!" the girls cheered.

Jason felt like he'd been punched in the stomach. He hadn't done anything, but still everyone hated him. *They hated him.*

"Maybe you can work on your behavior these next few weeks," Mrs. Kaplan suggested. "And by the end of the session, maybe somebody will give you another chance."

"Okay," Jason said, lowering his eyes. Somehow he felt responsible for everything Tank had done.

He was glad when Mrs. Kaplan finally changed the subject. "Today we'll start on the waltz," she said. "Let's listen to the music first so we can feel the rhythm of the dance. Then we'll try it."

Mrs. Kaplan pressed a button on the boom box and old-time music filled the gym.

Jason listened to the music. Dum da da, dum da da, dum da da.

At least he *tried* to listen. It was kind of hard when everyone kept shooting him angry looks.

Part of him wanted to shout out, "I'm not Tank Talbott! My name is Jason Pfeiffer, and I'm a nice kid. I don't do all that stuff that Tank did."

But Jason Pfeiffer didn't take ballroom dance class. Jason Pfeiffer took tadpole swimming. So for once, "Tank Talbott" kept his big mouth shut.

5
An Academy Award-Winning Performance

J ason had to admit, the dance class was actually kind of fun. Forward-side-together, back-side-together, he repeated to himself as he box-stepped his way to the bathroom after class.

He had gotten away with it! Everyone just assumed he was Tank Talbott. He wondered whether Tank had had such good luck in swimming class.

Where was Tank, anyway? Jason squinted at his watch. He hoped Tank wasn't beating someone up.

Jason pulled his movie script out of his backpack. He sat down on the floor, rubbed his eyes, then opened his notebook. Without his glasses, he had to hold the notebook right in front of his face. Now, where was I? Jason asked himself as he scanned through the last section he'd written. Oh, yeah. The part where the scientist traps the Dagmartian. He's got a big huge needle and he's about to plunge it into the Dagmartian to test her blood when suddenly...

Jason didn't know. Would the Dagmartian escape? Or would she attack the scientist?

While he was trying to make up his mind, Tank

burst into the bathroom. Water dripped from his wet head to Jason's towel, which was draped around Tank's shoulders.

"That was so cool!" he said, pushing Jason's glasses up on his nose as though they were his own. "I waited until the end like you said, and then I put my face in the water. Ms. Hall went crazy!"

Jason blinked. "Sh-she did?" he asked. He hugged his notebook to his chest and slowly rose to his feet.

Tank nodded. "She said, 'I knew you'd do it!' She even called over this other teacher and made him watch me—"

"Other teacher?" Jason's notebook fell to the floor. "What other teacher?"

"I don't know. Just some guy who knows you." Tank bent down and picked up Jason's notebook. "Hey, what's this? 'The Dagmartian,'" he read.

Jason snatched the notebook out of Tank's hand. "It's nothing!" he said. The last thing he needed was Tank flipping through the script and finding the Turbo-Tank scene.

"So, tell me about this other teacher," Jason said, changing the subject. "Did he have dark hair?" Mr. Abram had dark hair. Could they actually fool Mr. Abram?

"Gee, I don't know," Tank said in a high-pitched girly voice. "I couldn't see a thing without my glasses." He laughed at his own joke, then took off the glasses and handed them to Jason.

Jason put his glasses on. Ah. The world was clear again.

Tank gathered up the school clothes he had tossed in the corner before class and took them to the middle toilet stall. "I tell you, Dork Face, people were so amazed that I, er, you could put your face in the water! I felt like a movie star!"

"And everyone really thought you were me?" Jason asked through the closed door.

"Of course they did," Tank said. His wet swimming trunks hit the floor with a slap. "At first, I just stood there and whined *I can't do it! I can't put my face in the water!* I sounded just like you."

Jason watched Tank's legs disappear into a pair of jeans. He didn't think Tank sounded *anything* like him.

"I just sort of stood there and shivered like you probably would. And the teacher said, 'Try.' So I said, 'Okay. I'll try.' And then I lowered my head down really slow. I scrunched my eyes shut. I gritted my teeth and...I put my face in the water."

Tank came out of the stall. "It was an Academy Award-winning performance, Dork Face."

"And everyone really thought you were me?"

"I told you they did." Tank laughed. "I love pretending I'm a geek. So, how was the dance class?"

"Not bad," Jason said as he picked up his swimming trunks and wrung them out over the sink. "In fact, it was kind of fun."

Tank snorted. "You would think so. Hey, maybe you should get your hair wet under the sink or something so you look like you've been swimming."

Not a bad idea, Jason thought. "Maybe you should dry yours under the hand dryer," he told Tank.

Jason turned the hot and the cold taps until the water felt just right. Then he stuck his head in the sink and let the water wash over him. When he finished, he wiped the drops off his face, then combed his hair.

Tank picked up Jason's towel and dropped it over Jason's shoulders. "There," Tank said. "You look like you just got out of the pool."

Jason stared at his reflection in the mirror. *He did.* In fact, he almost looked like a real swimmer.

"Well, I should probably go," Jason said.

Tank nodded. "See you later, Dork Face." Then he punched the knob for the hand dryer and leaned his head under the spout.

Jason walked out of the bathroom and his heart stopped.

His mom was talking to his swimming teacher!

"I was just telling your mom what a great lesson you had today, Jason." Ms. Hall smiled.

Jason tried to smile back. Man, it was a good thing he'd wet his hair down. He didn't dare get too close to Ms. Hall.

"I knew that if we just gave it enough time, you'd put your face in the water," Mom said. "I'm so proud of you!" She squeezed his shoulders.

Proud? Mom was proud?

"Yo! Dork Face!" came a voice behind him. "Is that you?"

Jason turned. Was Tank crazy? Jason tilted his head toward the door as if to say, GET LOST, TANK!

Tank smiled. "See you in school!" He waved.

"Is that a friend of yours, Jason?" Mom asked. Ever since Luke moved away, Mom had been bugging him about making new friends.

"Who? That kid over there?" Jason let out a nervous laugh. "I've never seen him before in my whole life."

6
Celebrating

So, he put his face in the water. Big deal."
Dagmar stirred her cup of blueberry frozen
yogurt. "He's got a long way to go before he's
actually swimming."

"It's still a big deal." Mom smiled at Jason.

"Remember last summer?" Dad said.

"I don't want to talk about what happened last
summer!" Dagmar glared at Dad as she stabbed her
spoon into her yogurt.

"Well, honey, Jason had a lot of fear to work
through," Mom said. "Remember when he started lessons last fall? Remember how he screamed when they
tried to get him to put his face in the water?"

"But he kept trying and trying until finally he
could do it." Dad patted Jason on the back. "I think
that's worth celebrating."

Jason smiled weakly. He felt a little guilty about
all this fuss. After all, he hadn't really put his face in
the water. Tank had.

And now his whole family was going out for ice
cream to celebrate.

"Whatever." Dagmar shrugged.

She wasn't impressed because she could breathe with her face in the water just as easily as she could breathe with her face out of the water. It was like she was part human and part fish.

Hey, Jason thought. Part fish. That's good! What if the Dagmartian was part human and part fish?

"Quick! Someone get me some paper and a pen," Jason ordered. He had to get this down.

Mom opened her purse and rummaged through it. "I've got a pen, but I don't have any paper."

"That's okay," Jason said, grabbing the pen. "I'll just write it on napkins." He yanked a handful of napkins out of the dispenser.

Forget about the Dagmartian having two heads. She just had *one* head. A *fish* head. And that fish head sat on top of an otherwise human body. Jason was growing more excited by the minute.

Dagmar rolled her eyes. "Let me guess. More stupid ideas for your pathetic little movie?"

Everyone in Jason's family knew his movie was a scary movie. But no one knew exactly what it was about. "For your information, Dagmar," Jason said sweetly. "This movie is a future blockbuster!"

"Right," Dagmar said.

Jason leaned over his pile of napkins and started writing.

Celebrating

* * *

Jason worked on his script late into the night. Most of it was "director notes."

The Dagmartian is about eight feet tall, he wrote in his best handwriting. *She's gray with lots of green slime running down her body. She's got a head like a fish and a body like a human.* Boy, the Special Effects people would have a blast with this.

Jason flipped pages until he got to the part where the Dagmartian first appears. The scene is shot at a swimming pool.

Camera one pans the entire area. People talking, reading, lying on the deck chairs. There's three or four lifeguards, and people are in the pool laughing and splashing and having a good time.

Cut to camera two, which zooms in on the drain at the bottom of the pool. The music turns eerie. And something gray oozes up through the drain.

It's taking form. It's a fish. No, it's a human! Nobody knows what it is!

Suddenly there's a scream. Camera three focuses on a boy around ten years old who is holding his hands to his cheeks and screaming bloody murder.

Then a man in a red swimsuit speaks the first line. "What is it?"

That line's okay, Jason decided. But the rest needed

to go. Jason tore two whole pages out of his notebook, and crumpled them up. Then he started fresh.

"It's a big fish," Teen 1 says.

"It can't be a fish," Teen 2 replies. "It's got legs."

"It's some kind of mutant."

"Or a visitor from another planet!"

"It's almost nine o'clock," a voice called from downstairs. "Bedtime!"

Already? Jason groaned. But he knew Mom and Dad were probably watching TV. They wouldn't come up and make him turn out his light until the next commercial.

Jason looked back over his scene. Camera two zooms in on the Dagmartian. She raises her head up out of the water. Camera three shows all the people backing away in fear.

Jason stopped. Oh, this was his best idea yet! If the Dagmartian is part human, maybe she can speak?

Back to camera two. The creature opens her mouth and says, "I am the Dagmartian!"

"The Dagmar-tian?" said a voice that was not part of his movie.

Jason jumped as the real live Dagmartian pulled the notebook out from under his arm.

"Hey! That's mine!" Jason lunged for the notebook, but Dagmar held it out of his reach.

"A creature with a fish head and human body,"

Dagmar read with disbelief.

Oh, boy. He was in for it now.

"Give it back," Jason said, reaching for the notebook. Dagmar shoved him aside.

Jason watched her lips move as she read. Her eyes widened, then narrowed. Common sense told him he should run while he had the chance. But part of him wanted to see her full reaction.

"I suppose you think this is funny?" Dagmar looked up at him finally.

"No," Jason said in a serious voice. "I think it's scary. Very scary. It is a horror movie, after all."

Dagmar whacked him in the arm with his script. "Cute," she said. She tossed the notebook into the garbage can that sat beside Jason's desk.

"Mom and Dad say it's time to get ready for bed," she said. And with that, she left his room.

Jason rubbed his arm, but it didn't even hurt. That was it? Dagmar wasn't going to take him down and sit on him? She wasn't going to rip his teeth out one by one and stuff them down his throat? She wasn't going to do anything to him at all?

Jason figured he'd better watch his back. He knew Dagmar wouldn't just let this go. Sometime, when he least expected it, she'd get him back.

7
Jason, the Criminal

Mrs. Kaplan wasn't in the gym when Jason arrived on Tuesday. But a mint green sweater was draped over a chair at the front of the gym and the boom box was sitting on the floor.

Jason blinked to adjust his blurry vision. Most of the girls were already here. They stopped talking when Jason walked in and watched him like he was...well, like he was Tank.

Here we go again, Jason thought.

He didn't expect these girls to become his new best buds or anything. They were girls, after all. But did they have to treat him like a criminal?

"You'd better not try anything," one of them said, glaring at him. She wore jeans and a long sweater and she had a ponytail sticking out the side of her head.

"Yeah. Even though Mrs. Kaplan isn't here right now, we're in charge. Not you," another girl informed him.

"Yeah, whatever," Jason muttered.

"What did you say?" Ponytail asked in a tough voice.

"Nothing," Jason said. "I'm just standing here."

"Yeah, but you're probably thinking of trying something," the shortest girl spoke up.

"Hello, everyone." Mrs. Kaplan smiled as she sailed into the room. Her smile even included Jason. "How are you all?" Her tennis shoes made no sound at all as she walked over to the boom box.

"Fine," the girls chorused.

Jason didn't say anything.

"Good," Mrs. Kaplan smiled again. "Today we're going to start off by listening to some new music. It's a little different from the music we had last week, but it's still three-quarter time, so you can still waltz to it. Let's listen."

She pressed a button on the boom box and screaming guitars and drums blared through the speakers.

Mrs. Kaplan's eyes just about popped out of her head. She frowned and shut off the music.

A couple of the girls giggled.

"Is this somebody's idea of a joke?" Mrs. Kaplan's eyes fixed on Jason.

Everyone else turned to him, too.

"Hey, I didn't do it," he said.

"If you didn't, then who did?" a girl with a Save the Whales T-shirt asked.

"How should I know?" Jason asked. He turned to Mrs. Kaplan. "They were all here before I was. One of

41

them probably did it. And now they're trying to pin it on me."

Ponytail rolled her eyes. "Yeah, right."

"Yeah, right!" Jason repeated. "You all just want to see me get in trouble."

"Let's not argue." Mrs. Kaplan held up her hands. "We can dance without music today. But if this happens again..." She looked pointedly at Jason. "Somebody will find himself out of class."

"But I—"

"Tank!" Mrs. Kaplan shot him a warning look.

"—didn't do it," Jason whispered.

After class, Jason told Tank what had happened.

"Hey, way to go, Dork Face!" Tank laughed as he clapped Jason on the back. "Switching cassettes." He nodded his approval. "I never would have thought of that."

"But I didn't do it," Jason protested.

"Sure, you didn't," Tank said with a smirk.

Jason wrapped his swimsuit in his towel. He looked up at Tank. "H-h-have you been, you know, getting in trouble in swimming?"

"Who me?" Tank raised his voice an octave. "Little Jason Pfeiffer? No way. Little Jason Pfeiffer never gets in trouble."

Jason didn't know whether to believe Tank or not.

"Just remember," Tank said, waving his finger in

Jason's face. "If you get me kicked out of dance class, you'll have to go back to your swimming class." Then he tossed his head back and laughed.

* * *

Cool_Luke324: I bet Tank did it. I bet he switched the tapes.

Moviemaker: I don't think so. He thought it was funny when I told him. But I don't think he did it.

Cool_Luke324: I bet he did. It sounds like the kind of thing he'd do.

Moviemaker: No. I think it was one of the girls in the class.

Cool_Luke324: Why would they do that?

Moviemaker: To get me (TANK!) in trouble? They really hate Tank.

Cool_Luke324: Can you blame them?

"Dagmar! What are you doing?" Jason heard Mom cry from across the hall. Jason got up to see what was going on in Dagmar's room.

"Boxing up my swimming stuff," Dagmar said.

Mom reached into the box and pulled out one of Dagmar's trophies. "But these are all your awards."

Dagmar continued tossing stuff into the box.

"Just because you're not on the swim team anymore

doesn't mean you have to put away your awards," Mom said.

"I know. I just want to."

"But why, honey? You earned these awards. Why wouldn't you want to display them?"

"They're *my* awards! I don't have to display them if I don't want to!" Dagmar yelled as she slammed the box lid closed.

Jason took a step back. His sister was in one of her moods again. When she got like that, anything could happen.

"I don't understand—" Mom began.

Dagmar picked up her box. "Well, you don't have to understand! THESE ARE MY AWARDS AND THIS IS MY LIFE AND IF I WANT TO THROW THESE STUPID AWARDS IN THE GARBAGE THEN I CAN!" She stormed out.

Jason flattened himself against the wall as she stomped past him. But Dagmar didn't even look at him.

Was she really going to throw all her swimming awards away?

Mom looked at Jason and shrugged. All Jason could do was shrug back. At least Dagmar hadn't thrown her box of awards at him.

* * *

Jason decided he'd better get to dance class early

the next Thursday. He wanted to make sure no one did anything else to get him in trouble. Rather than hang around to chat with Tank, Jason simply handed Tank his glasses, then took off for the gym.

"Hey, Dork Face!" Tank called after him. "What's the rush? Can't wait to get back to all your girlfriends?"

Very funny, Jason thought as he rounded the corner into the gym.

Perfect. He was the first one here. He even beat Mrs. Kaplan. He turned on all the lights in the gym, then wandered around. The huge glass windows along the back wall looked out on the tennis courts.

He should have a building with windows like these in his movie. Maybe the Dagmartian could come crashing through and disrupt a really fancy dinner or dance...

"Tank?" Mrs. Kaplan's voice cut through his thoughts. "What are you doing here so early?"

Jason turned. He squinted. Mrs. Kaplan wore a pink sweater today. She carried the boom box in her hand and eyed Jason as though she didn't quite trust him. Even though he'd always been the perfect ballroom dance student.

"I uh, just couldn't wait to get here today," Jason said. "I couldn't wait to learn some new dance steps."

Mrs. Kaplan looked doubtful. "Tell me, Tank. Were you here early last time, too?"

Jason felt as though the floor had dropped out from under him. He knew what she was getting at. She wanted to know whether he was here early enough to switch the cassettes on her last time. Well, he was getting tired of everyone assuming the worst of him.

"I didn't switch the cassettes, Mrs. Kaplan," Jason said in his most polite voice. "Really, I didn't."

But Jason could tell Mrs. Kaplan didn't believe him.

8
Tank, the Idea Man

*P*oor *Tank*, Jason thought. Then he shook himself. Did he really think, poor *Tank?* It was Tuesday noon. Ever since Luke moved away, Jason had been eating lunch alone. He didn't mind, because it gave him time to work on his script. But lately, Tank had been sitting at the other end of Jason's table.

Usually Jason and Tank ignored each other. But for some reason today, Jason found himself watching Tank carefully string macaroni pieces onto his fork.

"What are you looking at?" Tank scowled.

"Nothing." Jason turned his attention back to his script. His goal was to finish Scene 25 during lunch. Scene 25 was the one where the Dagmartian chases a bus full of teachers. But for some reason, Jason couldn't keep his mind on his story. His thoughts kept wandering back to Tank.

Jason had been thinking about Tank a lot since last Thursday's dance class. He realized that even if Tank turned things around and started treating people better, it still would be a long time before anyone trusted him. People looked at Tank and saw a bully.

No matter what Tank was doing at the moment, that's what they saw.

"*What* are you staring at?" Tank asked again. This time he seemed ticked off.

"Nothing," Jason said. He didn't realize he'd still been staring.

"Are you drawing a goofy picture of me or something?" Tank stood up.

"I'm not drawing a picture of you," Jason said. "I'm just writing. See?" Jason held up his notebook. He hoped Tank would think it was just his class journal and leave him alone.

Tank turned back to his macaroni and cheese.

Jason looked down at his plate. Gloppy macaroni and cheese, overcooked beans, a half-eaten piece of bread, and chocolate pudding. Yuck. Jason decided he'd at least eat the pudding. Unfortunately, he'd forgotten to pick up a spoon. He went to get one.

"Watch where you're going, Tank!" a girl with wispy blond hair cried when Jason nearly collided with her.

"Sorry," Jason said as he hopped out of the way.

"Too bad I ate my chocolate pudding," she sneered at him as she dumped the remainder of her lunch into the trash can. "Otherwise I could've poured it over your head."

That was rude, Jason thought. Before he could

stop himself, he said, "Yeah, well, I still have my pudding. Maybe I should go get it and pour it over *your* head."

Whoa! That sounded like something Tank would say, not something I'd say, Jason thought.

"Go ahead," the girl said. She had one hand planted on her hip. "I'd like to see you try."

"Hey, I was just kidding," Jason said.

He stepped to go around the girl. Wait a minute. She looked a little familiar. And now she was looking at him kind of funny, too.

The dance class! That was where he'd seen her. That explained why she'd called him *Tank*. That's why it looked like she had darts in her eyes.

Don't say anything, Jason told himself. Just let her think you're Tank.

He went to get his spoon and then went back to his table. And his script.

But his script wasn't there.

He was sure he'd left it right beside his plate. But it wasn't there. Where was it?

Jason checked his chair. He checked under the table. Panic rose in his throat. *Where could it be?*

"This is really stupid!" came a voice from the other end of the table.

Tank. Not only did he have Jason's script, *he was actually reading it, too.*

"Give that back!" Jason said, reaching for it.

Tank turned his back to Jason and kept reading.

Jason's heart raced as he thought about Scene 2. The Turbo-Tank scene. That was quite a ways back in his notebook, so Tank *probably* wasn't reading it. But what if he was?

Finally Tank slid the notebook back down the table. "It wasn't too bad until I realized the Dagmartian was part human, part fish. Then it's like, big deal. She's a mermaid!"

Jason blinked.

"I mean, I thought the Dagmartian was this really scary monster. Worse than Frankenstein!" Tank shoved a forkful of macaroni into his mouth, then continued, chewing while he talked. "But it turns out she's just a *mermaid.*"

Jason cleared his throat. "B-b-but a mermaid has a human head and a fish body. M-m-my Dagmartian has a fish head and a human body." Not that he cared what Tank thought.

Tank shrugged. "I still say she's a mermaid. I think instead of having the Dagmartian come out of a swimming pool, you should have her come out of a sewer," he said. "Or maybe you could make her come out of some guy's stomach. You know. Like they did in *Alien.* You could make her really slimy and gross—"

"I'll think about it," Jason interrupted. He sure

didn't want to talk about it. Not with Tank, anyway. He closed his notebook and shoved it under his tray.

"Wait, there's more," Tank said.

"More?"

Tank nodded. "I think you need to give the creature a different name."

"What's wrong with the Dagmartian?"

"Well, no one believes in Martians anymore," Tank said. "And there isn't any water on Mars. Not for swimming in, anyway. Yet you have her attacking all these people in the water. It doesn't make sense. If the Dagmartian comes from a place where there aren't lakes and swimming pools, she wouldn't be able to swim any better than you."

Jason bit his lip. He had to admit Tank had a point there.

"You keep thinking about this stuff," Tank said as he pushed his chair back. "We'll talk more at the Rec Center."

Jason frowned. What did Tank mean they'd talk *more*? What did Tank know about making movies, anyway?

But as the day wore on, a couple of the things Tank said nagged at Jason like a pebble inside his tennis shoe.

He never thought about where the Dagmartian came from. A DagMARTIAN probably did come from

Mars. But that just didn't work at all.

After school, Tank met Jason in the Rec Center bathroom. "So, did you change your movie script?" Tank asked right away. "I want to see."

Jason hugged his backpack tighter to his chest. "I uh, haven't made any changes. Not yet, anyway," he added when he saw the look on Tank's face.

Tank went into a bathroom stall. "Well, maybe I should take your notebook home after class and read the whole thing—"

"No!" Jason cried. Tank couldn't read the whole thing. He absolutely couldn't!

"Dork Face," Tank said in a warning voice. "If I want to read the whole thing, I'm going to. Besides, I'm an idea guy. I'll probably come up with all kinds of great ideas for you."

Great. Just what Jason needed. More ideas from Tank Talbott.

9
Partners

Jason's heart wasn't in his dancing today. When everyone else moved forward, he moved forward. And when everyone else moved back, he moved back. But his feet were on autopilot, and his mind was on the Dagmartian.

He was going to have to start all over with a whole new creature. A Dagmar-something-else, he thought as he moved forward-side-together, back-side-together.

Whatever the Dagmar-something-else turned out to be, it had to be something that bubbled up through the drain in the bottom of a swimming pool.

Forward-side-together. Back-side-together.

"Very nice, Tank," Mrs. Kaplan smiled as she made her way around the room. She hugged the pink sweater that was draped over her shoulders. "Good posture. Nice rhythm. I knew you could do this if you put your mind to it."

Jason could hardly believe it. This was the first time he hadn't really paid attention in dance class, and yet this was the first time Mrs. Kaplan had paid him a compliment.

"Uh, thanks," he said.

The music stopped and Mrs. Kaplan made her way to the front of the group. "Okay," she said. "I think we're ready to try it with partners now."

Mrs. Kaplan looked around the gym. "I see we have an even number today," she said, tapping her finger against her chin. "Wouldn't *somebody* like to dance with Tank?"

Jason glanced warily around the room. The girls groaned.

"Come on, now. We didn't have any trouble with Tank last time, and I'm sure we won't have any trouble with him today, either. Will we, Tank?" Mrs. Kaplan asked.

Jason opened his mouth, then closed it again. What difference did it make what he said? These girls though he was a bully.

"Somebody?" Mrs. Kaplan glanced hopefully around the group. "Anybody?"

"Oh, forget it," Jason said. "I don't want to dance with any of them, anyway."

Maybe instead of a Dagmartian he should just make his creature an eleven-headed *girl*. One head would be his sister's and the other ten would be the girls from this dance class.

"I'll do it," came a voice from the back. "I'll be Tank's partner."

Jason turned. Who said that?

The girl stepped forward. It was that girl from lunch the other day. The one who wanted to pour pudding over his head. She smiled boldly at Jason.

Jason swallowed hard. Not her. Anyone but her.

"Ooooh, Kelly!" a couple of the other girls giggled.

"Kelly and Tank, sitting in a tree," someone sang.

"K-I-S-S-I-N-G," the others chimed in.

Kelly glared at them. "You're acting stupid!"

Jason's cheeks burned.

"Okay, that's enough," Mrs. Kaplan said. She started the music again. "Let's get into position."

Jason felt as though the floor had dropped out beneath him. He was going to have to *touch* a girl. He was going to have to hold Kelly's hands. Both of them. At the same time.

The music started.

Jason's feet moved. So did Kelly's. But their arms remained planted at their sides.

"Come on, you two," Mrs. Kaplan said, coming up behind Jason. "This is ballroom dancing. You have to hold hands." She grabbed one of Jason's hands and one of Kelly's hands and clasped them together.

Kelly's hand felt cold. His own hand felt damp.

"Don't worry, Kelly. Tank will behave today." She looked at him pointedly. "Won't you, Tank?"

"Yes, I'll behave!" he said through gritted teeth. How many times would he have to keep saying it?

"Good." Mrs. Kaplan smiled. "You both have the footwork down. Now all you have to do is relax."

Relax? How was he supposed to relax?

Forward-side-together. Back-side-together.

Mrs. Kaplan strolled over to the next pair of dancers.

Forward-side-together. Back-side-together.

Kelly cleared her throat. "This is kind of fun."

"Yeah," Jason agreed.

Kelly had the biggest, brownest eyes Jason had ever seen. She smiled. "A lot of people think ballroom dancing is kind of dumb."

"It's not dumb," Jason said right away.

Kelly gave him a goofy look. A look like the ones people in those old movies give each other right before they kiss.

Jason's stomach lurched. He didn't want to be kissed. Not by Kelly. Not by *anyone*.

Kelly opened her mouth.

No, he thought with growing horror as he took a step back. Don't do it. *Please don't do it*.

But Kelly didn't kiss him. She took a deep breath and said, "You're not really Tank Talbott, are you?"

10
We've Got Problems

Jason banged open the bathroom door. "We've got problems," he announced.

Tank snorted. "What problems?" he asked as he headed for the row of stalls.

Jason was right on his heels. "This girl, Kelly? She knows! She knows I'm not you!"

Tank went into the middle stall and locked it. "How do you know she knows?"

"Her exact words were, 'You're not really Tank Talbott, are you?' What are we going to do, Tank?"

"What did you say?" Tank sounded pretty calm behind that bathroom stall.

"I didn't say anything," Jason said, pacing back and forth. "Not at first. She said, 'Don't worry. I won't tell anyone—'"

"Great," Tank said. "Problem solved. Now, let's talk about our movie—"

"TANK!"

"What?" The toilet stall opened and Tank came out wearing his jeans and his Darth Vader shirt. His feet were still bare.

"The problem is *not* solved," Jason said nervously.

"You should've heard her. She wanted to know who I was, why I was taking your place, where you were——"

"Well, you didn't tell her any of that, did you?" Tank started towel-drying his hair.

Jason looked down at the tile floor. "I sort of told her my name."

"What? WHY?" Tank exploded. "Why didn't you just say 'I don't know what you're talking about, woman! I am *too* Tank Talbott!'"

Jason shrugged. "I don't know." He hadn't thought of that.

"Would it really kill you to tell a little white lie?" Tank asked.

"Why should I lie? She goes to our school. I think she's a fourth grader. She saw us at lunch the other day. That was how she knew I wasn't you."

What she'd said was: "the *real* Tank Talbott would never have said, 'just kidding.' *He* would've dumped his pudding over my head."

"Well, I don't know what we can do," Tank said. "But no way am I going back to that stupid dance class!"

Tank punched the button on the hair drier and stuck his head under the blower.

Jason crouched down to look Tank in the eye.

"Are you sure no one in the swimming class has figured it out, too?"

Tank stood up. "Positive," he said. Then he grinned. "But speaking of swimming...guess what? You're starting to learn the crawl stroke."

Any other time, Jason would have been thrilled. But right now, he was too scared. If they weren't careful, they were going to get caught.

Tank picked up his socks, then sat down beside Jason's backpack to put them on. "Relax, Dork Face. We're not going to get caught. Now, let's talk about our movie. Have you decided where else that monster could come from besides Mars?"

Our movie?

"Well, have you?" Tank asked.

Jason slid to the floor beside Tank. "Not yet."

"Then I guess I'll have to take your notebook home and figure it out myself," Tank said with a tsk-tsk sound. He grabbed Jason's backpack.

"No!" Jason lunged for his backpack.

But Tank already had the notebook. "What do you mean, *no?*" He glowered at Jason.

Jason couldn't let Tank read the part about the Turbo-Tank. But he also knew that letting Tank see him sweat would only make things worse. "I mean, why don't you let me take the script home and once I figure out how to fix it, *then* you can read it."

"Uh-uh." Tank held the notebook out of Jason's reach. "I want to read it, and I want to read it *now!*

This movie is going to make us both a ton of money!"

Jason blinked. "Both?"

"Yeah, *both!*" Tank said firmly. "You'll be the movie maker and I'll be your agent."

"What's an agent?" Jason asked.

Tank sighed. "I thought you knew how the movie business worked." He tucked Jason's notebook inside his gym bag and zipped it up.

Jason gulped.

"An agent is the guy who sells you," Tank went on. "Don't you ever watch TV? One day, people will ask us how we got together. And we'll tell them all about the dance lessons and the swimming lessons."

"We will?" Jason asked uneasily.

"Of course we will. It'll be great press." Tank slapped Jason's back. "From now on, it's you and me, Dork Face. You and me."

Jason gaped at Tank. It almost sounded like Tank had said the two of them were, well...friends.

Of course, Tank didn't know about the Turbo-Tank yet. Once he got to that part in the script, they wouldn't be friends. They wouldn't be anything because Jason would be dead.

11
The Waiting Game

After dinner, Jason lay on his bed and stared at his ceiling. He didn't think Tank would come all the way over here and beat him up tonight. He'd probably wait until school tomorrow. Which meant—Jason checked his watch—he had approximately twelve hours left to live.

While he was planning his funeral, the phone rang.

Jason held his breath. What if it was Tank? What if Tank wanted to beat him up right now?

"Jason! Phone!" Dagmar yelled from across the hall.

Jason bolted up in his bed. It *was* Tank.

"Tell him I can't come to the phone," Jason yelled back. "Tell him I moved to Alaska and didn't leave a forwarding number!"

Dagmar threw Jason's bedroom door open. "Forget it. I'm not going to lie for you. Here." Dagmar thrust the cordless phone at him.

She even smiled. What? Did Tank actually *tell* Dagmar he was going to beat Jason up? Did he tell her she could help?

"Say hello!" Dagmar hissed. "It's not polite to keep a girl waiting."

"Girl?" *What girl?*

Jason slowly raised the phone to his ear. "Uh, hello?" he said, glancing uneasily at his sister.

"Jason?" It wasn't a voice he recognized.

"Who's this?" Jason asked. Dagmar watched him expectantly.

"Kelly."

"Kelly who?"

"Kelly Sears. From dance class."

"Oh," Jason said, surprised. He rolled to his stomach. "What do you want?" he whispered into the receiver.

"Um, well, I just wanted to explain. You know. About the cassette tapes at dance class."

"You're the one who switched them?" Jason knew it. He *knew* it had been one of those girls.

"It was Yolanda and Lauren's idea. They brought the tape. But they were too chicken to make the switch. So I did it."

"Oh." Jason had to be careful what he said with Dagmar still hanging around.

"We thought you were Tank!" Kelly went on. "We just wanted to get back at him for all the mean stuff he did to us. If we had known it was you, we wouldn't have done it."

62

"Uh-huh," Jason said. He didn't know whether to believe her or not.

"Really, we wouldn't have!" Kelly insisted. "We like you, Jason. We want you to keep coming to class."

We? Jason sat up. "You mean other people know about this, too?"

"Just Yolanda and Lauren. They won't tell."

Oh, *sure.*

"Besides, I had to tell them," Kelly said. "Otherwise they might have done something else to you."

Jason swallowed. He wouldn't have wanted that.

"The main thing is, we don't want Mrs. Kaplan to find out, right?" Kelly said. "If she finds out, then we'll be stuck with Tank again."

"That's right," Jason said. That was a good point and he hoped those girls would remember it.

"Why are you doing this for him, anyway?" Kelly asked. "Are you guys friends or something?"

Jason snorted. "Not exactly."

"Is he paying you to do it?"

"You could say that," Jason said. Dagmar sat down beside him on the bed.

"Is he paying you a lot?"

"Sort of." Jason wished his sister would get lost. It was hard enough talking to a girl on the phone. But it was ten times worse with Dagmar hanging around, twirling her hair around her finger.

Kelly sighed. "You're not going to tell me the real story, are you?"

"Nope."

"That's okay. Girls have ways of finding things out. See you on Thursday."

"What was *that* about?" Dagmar started bugging him as soon as he hung up the phone.

"Nothing."

She stood in front of him, blocking his way. "Is there anything you want to talk about?"

Jason's heart stopped. "What do you mean?" Did Dagmar suspect something? Was she trying to get him to confess so she wouldn't have to break a nail beating it out of him?

"I don't know. A girl calls you on the phone. I just thought you might want to talk about it."

"With you?" Jason would rather swallow rat poison.

Dagmar rolled her eyes. "I don't know why I even bother."

"Neither do I," Jason said.

* * *

The sun warmed Jason's back as he walked to school on Wednesday morning. He stopped to take off his jacket, then continued on his way. He wasn't in any hurry. The sooner he got to school, the sooner his life would be over. But when he got to school, he was surprised. Tank simply walked past Jason, his head buried in Jason's notebook.

He wasn't finished reading yet?

Well, it was sixty-five pages long. It took a while to read sixty-five pages. But the Turbo-Tank appeared in the second scene. Surely Tank had read that much by now?

At lunch, Jason sat at the opposite end of the table from Tank. Waiting. But Tank was still reading.

Tank continued to read during science and social studies and current events. Would he *ever* finish? And what would he do to Jason when he did?

"What is so fascinating, Mr. Talbott?" their teacher, Mr. Burns, asked. He always called people by their last names.

Twenty-five heads whirled around to look at Tank.

Tank looked up. "Huh? Oh, you mean this?" He held up Jason's notebook.

Jason dropped his head to his desk. The next thing he knew, Mr. Burns would be reading his script, too. And probably marking all over it with his red pen. At least there wasn't a Mr. Burns sort of monster in the script.

"It's just a story," Tank said.

"Well, I'd appreciate it if you'd read your story outside of class," Mr. Burns said. "Right now we're discussing current events."

Tank closed Jason's notebook and put it away. He didn't even look Jason's way. Maybe he didn't realize the Turbo-Tank was based on him. Or maybe he had gotten caught up in the story. Maybe he even *liked* the story. But that was pushing it a little.

Jason was surprised to discover he actually cared what Tank thought. And it wasn't just that he was worried about getting beaten up. Tank was the first person to read the entire script. He really wanted Tank to tell him it was good. In fact, he wanted Tank to drop to Jason's feet in awe and say, "Wow! I've never read anything so great in my entire life!"

After school, Jason was walking home when he heard a voice behind him. "Hey, Dork Face!"

Tank.

Jason stopped. He turned and saw Tank running toward him, waving the red notebook.

"I did it," Tank said, his chest heaving as he tried to catch his breath. "I read the whole thing."

Tank didn't look like he was going to kill him. At least, not yet.

"It's really long," Tank said. They started walking again.

"Yeah, I know."

"I mean, *really* long. Don't you think it's about time to write, 'The End'?"

"The end?" Jason said. He hadn't thought about

ending his movie yet. He was having too much fun simply coming up with new people for the Dagmartian to attack.

"And guess what?" Tank said as they crossed a street. "I have the perfect ending for you."

"You do?"

"Yup. But first you have to get rid of Scene 2."

Jason gulped. Scene 2 was the Turbo-Tank scene.

"Then in your last scene..." Tank opened the notebook and turned to the last page of writing. "Scene 28, *that's* where you can bring out the Turbo-Tank."

"Y-you like the Turbo-Tank?" Jason asked.

"Oh, yeah!" Tank cried. "He's going to be like your secret weapon! And this last scene is going to be awesome. The Turbo-Tank is going to defeat the Dagmartian. Or whatever we decide to call her. There'll be blood and guts. Explosions and fireballs. What do you think, Dork Face?"

Jason didn't know. *The Dagmartian* had to end sometime. And however it ended, something would have to defeat the Dagmartian. But the Turbo-Tank? Jason had never thought of that.

It wasn't a bad idea, though. Not bad at all.

"I want you to write that scene the minute you get home from school," Tank said, closing the notebook. "And then as soon as you finish, call me and read it to me over the phone." He yanked Jason's notebook out of Jason's hands and wrote his phone number on the cover.

"Um, okay," Jason said as he took the notebook back.

"We still need to talk about a new name for the Dagmartian, too," Tank said. "What have you come up with?"

"Uh, well…" Jason said. He hadn't come up with anything he liked as much as he liked the Dagmartian. "How about the Dagmaniac?" he said after a few minutes.

Tank shook his head. "Not scary enough."

"How about the Dagmarinator?"

Tank frowned. "Sounds too much like *The Terminator*."

"So? *The Terminator* was a good movie."

"Your parents let you watch *The Terminator*?" Tank's eyebrows shot up.

"Well, not exactly," Jason admitted. "But I know what it's about."

"Yeah, well, your monster is more of a…a *blob* than anything. She sort of sucks up everything in her way."

"True," Jason gave in. He thought some more. "Hey, how about the Dagmablob?"

"That's good!" Tank nodded. "Now, go home and write that last scene. Don't forget to call me as soon as you're done."

Jason half-walked, half-danced the rest of the way home.

Tank liked his movie! And Tank wasn't easy to please. Maybe Jason really would be a movie maker when he grew up? And maybe, just maybe, Tank would be his agent?

Whoa! That would be weird.

12
The End

The little red light on the phone was blinking when Jason got home. Jason wanted to get right upstairs, but he pressed the Play Messages button just in case that girl Kelly had called again and left him a message. If she did, Jason sure wouldn't want anyone else to hear it.

Beep! "Hello? Jason?" It was Luke. Jason let out the breath he didn't realize he was holding. "Just wondering what you're up to lately," Luke said. "Call me, okay?" Jason knew it had been awhile since he'd instant messaged Luke. He wanted to call him back. But he also wanted to finish his script.

He went upstairs and cleared off his desk and sat down. First he went through his entire script and changed all the Dagmartians to Dagmablobs. Then he started writing that last scene.

Jason thought he'd be working on *The Dagmartian*—er, *The Dagmablob*—until he grew up. Or at least until his sister grew up. But Tank was right. It was time to end *The Dagmablob*. That way he'd be free to start on another movie. Maybe *The Dagmablob Returns*?

Oh yes. A movie like *The Dagmablob* practically

demanded a sequel.

Jason would have to be careful with the end. He needed to make the audience think the Dagmablob was dead, but he also had to make sure it was possible to bring her back.

Maybe she could get blown up with dynamite? Then, in *The Dagmablob Returns*, all those little blown up pieces of blob would grow. It wouldn't be just one Dagmablob returning. It would be hundreds of them. Thousands of them.

Jason shivered. Talk about scary!

But the last scene still had to have the Turbo-Tank somehow.

Jason chewed on the end of his pencil and thought some more. How could the Turbo-Tank defeat the Dagmablob? How do you fight a blob, anyway?

Maybe the Turbo-Tank could somehow suck the Dagmablob inside himself? Yeah, that would work! There could be this big fight where the Dagmablob first tries to break apart the Turbo-Tank, but she doesn't succeed. Then the Turbo-Tank tries to vacuum the Dagmablob up inside himself. Back and forth until everyone in the audience is sitting on the edge of their chairs, wondering who's going to win.

Of course the Turbo-Tank does. In this movie anyway. In the next movie, the Turbo-Tank could just sort of vomit the Dagmablob back up. Tank would love it

71

because it would mean the Turbo-Tank would appear in *The Dagmablob Returns.*

"I am so good!" Jason sang out loud as he wrote the final scene. Words poured from his brain, down his arm and out his pencil.

And then he was done.

"Wow," Jason breathed as he gazed at those words, The End. I did it! he thought. I wrote a real screenplay! From start to finish.

Jason felt like this was the beginning of the rest of his life. He put his pencil down, stood up and started be-bopping all around the room.

Then he stopped.

Be cool, he reminded himself. Steven Spielberg probably doesn't be-bop. He probably...*waltzes!*

Jason imagined himself all dressed up in a black tuxedo with tails. He had just received his Academy Award and was at a celebration dinner where people were waltzing. *Good thing he knew how to waltz!*

Jason reached for his blue notebook. "May I have this dance?" he asked the notebook in a formal voice.

Forward-side-together. Back-side-together. Forward-side-together. Back-side-together.

I-am-good. I-am-good, Jason thought as his feet moved in perfect square boxes. I-am-good. I-am-good.

"Jason!" his mother's voice interrupted his fantasy. She stood in his doorway with a pile of clean towels and gaped at him. "Where did you learn to waltz?"

Jason stopped. "Uh..." he said.

"Did you learn that in gym class?" Mom asked, smiling at him.

"Yeah, that's it! I learned it in gym," Jason replied. He had learned it in a gym, anyway.

"That's wonderful!"

She went to put away the towels. Jason plopped down on his bed and breathed a sigh of relief.

But he still had to call Tank and read the final scene to him. He grabbed his notebook and went to the kitchen. He helped himself to a brownie from the pan on the stove for luck, then went to the phone. With a shaky finger he punched in Tank's number.

Tank picked up on the first ring. "It's about time you finished," he said. "What have you got?"

Jason wiped his sticky chocolate fingers on his jeans so he wouldn't get his script dirty. Then he opened to Scene 28 and started reading.

Dagmar came into the kitchen. She opened the pantry door and reached inside for a can of Diet Coke.

She must not have noticed him, so Jason cleared his throat and continued reading, louder this time. "Camera two zooms in on the Dagmablob as she opens her mouth—"

Dagmar whirled around. "Oh, now it's the *Dagmablob*? What happened to the *Dagmartian*?"

Jason kept reading. He tried not to smile. "The Turbo-Tank breathes fire and takes slow giant steps toward the Dagmablob. Then his twelve-foot-long tongue shoots out and wraps around the Dagmablob, squeezing her. Green blood oozes out through her eyes, ears, and mouth. But somehow she manages to escape."

Dagmar shook her head in disgust. "You are really warped, you know that?" She turned on her heel and left.

Jason grinned. "Hey, thanks!" he called after her.

"Come on, come on!" Tank cried. "The Dagmablob escapes. Then what?"

Jason read the rest of the scene to Tank. When he finished, Tank was quiet.

Uh-oh. That wasn't a good sign. "You don't like it?"

"Are you kidding?" Tank said. "It's awesome!"

"Really?"

"You know what we should do now?" Tank said. "We should send this to a real movie studio."

"Do you think so?"

"Definitely," Tank replied. "Can you go to the library Saturday? People who work at the library know everything, so I bet they could tell us where to send it."

"Okay!" Jason said. *Hollywood.* This was his dream. He knew he'd get there someday; he didn't expect to get there yet. Not when he was just eleven years old.

13
Mortimer Caldwell

On Friday night, Jason lay across his bed, fantasizing about his life as a rich and famous filmmaker, when Dagmar burst into his room.

"Mom and Dad went to a movie," she said. "So I was thinking...maybe you and I could...play a game or something."

Jason just about fell off his bed. "*You* want to play a game with *me*?"

He and Dagmar never played games together. They never did anything together. Except fight.

"Sure, why not?" Dagmar said.

Jason could think of a thousand reasons why not. Number one being, they didn't like each other.

Jason sat up on his bed. "What kind of game?" A beat-up Jason game?

Dagmar shrugged. "I don't know. Monopoly. Parcheesi. Something like that."

Monopoly? Parcheesi? When was the last time Dagmar played Monopoly or Parcheesi with anyone, much less with him? There had to be a catch.

"Well? Do you?" Dagmar asked.

"I don't know. I'm still thinking about it."

Dagmar rolled her eyes. "Oh, forget it! Forget I even asked!" She stomped across the hall to her room and slammed her door.

* * *

On Saturday morning, Tank rang Jason's doorbell at 8:15.

"What are you doing here so early?" Jason asked. "The library isn't even open yet."

"It'll open pretty soon," Tank said. "Come on."

They arrived at the library at 8:45. Fifteeen minutes before it opened. A librarian with curly brown hair took pity on them and let them in early. "You boys must have some important work to do," she said.

"We do," Tank said. "We need to find out where to send a movie script we've written."

"You boys have written a movie script?" The librarian looked impressed.

"Uh-huh," Tank said. "So now we need names and addresses of movie producers. Can you give us some?"

"Well," she said to Tank. "I've seen a book in the reference section that might help you. It's called the *Screen Writer's Market*." She led them into one of the aisles of shelves and stopped about halfway down. "Here we are," she said, pulling out a thick red volume and handing it to Jason.

"Thanks!" Jason said.

Tank took the book right out of Jason's hands and went to a back table to open it up. "Wow. Look at all these names and addresses. Which one should we go with?"

"Steven Spielberg," Jason said.

"Steven Spielberg?" Tank laughed. "Steven Spielberg is not going to look at a script from a nobody like you."

"Why not?"

"He just isn't. You need to start with someone who isn't already famous. But someone who knows a good script when he sees one. Someone who's hungry for new talent. Like this guy." Tank pointed at a name in the middle of the page.

"Mortimer Caldwell?" Jason wrinkled his nose.

"Doesn't he sound hungry?"

"He sounds like an old guy with a bad back."

"I think he sounds experienced. And with a name like Mortimer, I bet he does tons of horror movies."

Jason sniffed. "I've never heard of him."

"And he's never heard of you." Tank slapped his leg. "So, that's perfect."

"I don't know," Jason said. He wasn't sure he liked the idea of sending his precious script out to some guy he'd never even heard of.

"Well, I'm the agent, so you have to take my advice," Tank said. "And my advice is send it to this guy."

Jason sighed. "Okay." You couldn't argue with Tank.

Tank tore a sheet of paper from the back of Jason's notebook. Jason watched as Tank wrote "Dear Mr. Caldwell" in careful cursive writing. Tank stopped. "What should we say?"

Jason shrugged. "You're the agent."

Tank tapped his pencil. Then he started writing again. "My client, Jazz Fire—"

"Jazz Fire?" Jason interrupted.

"Your pen name," Tank explained. "It's more interesting than Jason Pfeiffer."

Jazz Fire was pretty, well...*jazzy*. But Jason always thought it would be his own name he saw in lights.

"My client, Jazz Fire, has written a script that's going to make you, me, and him a ton of money," Tank wrote. "So tell your secretary to hold all your calls. Then sit down and read *The Dagmablob* from start to finish right now. You won't be sorry. Signed, Thomas N. Talbott."

"Thomas N. Talbott? What does the N. stand for?" Jason wanted to know.

Tank slapped his hands down over the signature. "None of your business."

"Oh, come on. Tell me."

"No. You already saw my first name. And you better not tell anyone what it is!" Tank jabbed his index finger into Jason's chest.

"Why? What's wrong with Thomas?"

Tank sighed. "If you keep this up, Dork Face, I'm going to walk. You'll have to find somebody else to be your agent. You don't want that, do you?"

Jason thought for a minute. He had no idea whether he really needed an agent. And if he did, he seriously doubted another eleven-year-old was the right choice. But it sure was fun pretending with Tank.

"No," Jason said. "I don't mind you being my agent."

"Okay, then," Tank said. "Don't mention my real name again, and we should get along just fine."

14
Here Goes Nothing

O n the way to the Rec Center on Tuesday, Tank showed Jason a large manila envelope with the words URGENT, OPEN AT ONCE written all over it. It was addressed to Mr. Mortimer Caldwell. "I put your notebook in here along with my letter and a self-addressed stamped envelope addressed to me," Tank said. "That's what that screenwriter's book said to do."

"Sure," Jason said. "But why is the self-addressed stamped envelope addressed to you instead of to me?"

"Because I'm the agent!" Tank said. "And I paid for the stamps."

"I would've paid for the stamps," Jason grumbled.

"Dork Face..." Tank raised his eyebrow, but then his look softened. "Tell you what," he said as they stopped in front of the mail box outside the Rec Center. He handed Jason the envelope. "I'll let you mail it."

Jason held the package carefully in his hands like it was a tiny baby. He hated to let it go. But he knew that if he ever wanted *The Dagmablob* to get made into a real movie, he had to send it off.

"Here goes nothing," he said, dropping the package into the box. It hit the bottom with a thud.

"Here goes nothing," Tank agreed.

Then they went inside the Rec Center.

They didn't talk much when they were in the bathroom. Without *The Dagmablob*, what was there to talk about?

"See you after class," Jason said, handing Tank his glasses.

"See you after class," Tank echoed.

The minute Jason walked into the gym, a girl with straight black hair practically knocked him over. "Can I be your partner today, *Tank*?" she begged.

Two other girls were right on her heels. "No, I want to be *Tank's* partner," said one.

"No, me," said the other.

Jason stepped back. What was the deal with these girls looking at him, talking to him, *touching* him?

"I said it first!" The girl with the black hair reached for Jason's hand, but he pulled back before she actually touched him.

"Maybe he doesn't want to be your partner, Ashley." The girl with curly brown hair ran around to Jason's other side and grabbed his other hand. Jason yanked it away.

Ashley laughed. "Looks like he doesn't want to be your partner, either, Simone!"

"Whose partner *do* you want to be, *Tank*?" another girl asked.

Four pairs of eyes stared anxiously at him.

"Oh, no!" Jason slapped his forehead. So much for Kelly only telling two people about him. "You all know, don't you?" Probably the whole class knew.

They giggled. What an annoying sound. Like when Jason tried to play the violin and he couldn't get the strings to work right.

"Don't worry." Simone patted his back. "Your secret's safe with us."

Right. "I'm a dead man," Jason moaned.

"No, you're not," Kelly said, joining them. "I told you, we don't want the real Tank to come back." The others nodded.

Mrs. Kaplan came in then and plugged in her boom box. "Let's partner up," she said.

Five girls latched on to Jason at once. It was almost enough to make him wish he were back in tadpole swimming. Almost, but not quite.

Mrs. Kaplan turned. "Well, this is a surprise!" She put her glasses on so she could get a better look. "How nice that you all want to dance with Tank! Maybe you girls could take turns?"

So Jason danced with Ashley first. Then Simone. Then Kelly.

"See, Tank?" Mrs. Kaplan smiled at him. "Isn't it

nice when all the girls want to dance with you?"

Oh yeah. *Real* nice, Jason thought.

"Make sure you pick up one of those blue sheets of paper on your way out," Mrs. Kaplan said after class. She pointed to a stack of papers that were sitting on the floor by the door.

"See you next time, *Tank!*" Yolanda called.

"Goodbye, *Tank!*" Ashley winked at him.

"It was fun dancing with you, *Tank.*"

Mrs. Kaplan walked with him towards the door. "I'm so glad you've turned your behavior around, Tank," she said. "Those first couple of lessons were pretty rough."

First *couple*? Jason thought. Tank had only been there for one class. So how was it the first *couple* of classes were rough?

"But I see an obvious difference in your attitude now. And so do the girls."

Yeah, the difference is they found out I'm a whole different person, Jason thought.

"As you go through life, you'll find that when you're nice to other people, they'll usually be nice to you, too." Mrs. Kaplan looked at him over the tops of her glasses.

"Uh-huh." Jason smiled weakly.

By this time, they'd reached the door. "Oops. Don't forget one of these." Mrs. Kaplan picked up a blue paper and handed it to Jason.

"Thanks," he said. As he headed down the hall toward the bathroom, he glanced at the paper.

Dear Parents,
Your students have been working extra
hard in ballroom dance class and we would
like to take this opportunity to invite you to
our end-of-class ball.

ARRGH!!!!!! Jason ran the rest of the way to the bathroom.

Two of the three bathroom stall doors were closed. Jason peered underneath. There was no one in the end stall. But Jason's swimming trunks lay in a heap on the floor under the middle stall. And the person in there was stepping into a pair of jeans.

Jason pounded on the door. "Tank? We've got another problem. Our last class is in two weeks and Mrs. Kaplan is having an end-of-class *ball!*"

"So?"

"So, *parents* are invited! I've got the invitation right here. You're supposed to take it home to your folks."

The toilet stall banged open. "Do I have to do all the thinking around here?" Tank asked.

Jason took a step back.

"Why would I invite *my* folks to *your* little Cinderella's ball? Huh?" He yanked the invitation out of Jason's hand and ripped it into tiny pieces.

Jason looked down at the floor. "Yeah, but everyone else's parents are going to be there," he said. "Don't you think people will wonder why my parents aren't there?"

"Just tell Mrs. Kaplan your parents can't get off work," Tank said. "Some parents can't get time off, you know."

The end toilet stall banged open.

Jason jumped. A really scary-looking kid who was probably in junior high came out of the stall. Had he been hiding in there all along?

The guy had on black jeans, a black jacket, and an earring in his left ear. He blew his long black hair out of his face. Then he folded his arms across his chest and grinned a sideways grin at Tank.

"Yeah, but *your* parents definitely would take time off, wouldn't they, *Thomas?*"

15
Deep Doo-Doo

*T*homas? "Do you know this guy?" Jason asked Tank.

"Of course Thomas-the-Tank knows me," the older boy grinned as he walked over toward Tank and pulled him in a head-lock.

Thomas-the-*Tank*? As in that little kid's show about the blue train? That was where Tank got his nickname?

"I'm the Tank's brother, Zack," he said. He looked at Tank the same way Dagmar looked at Jason. Like his whole purpose in life was to torture him.

"I knew something was up," Zack said, tightening his hold on Tank. "You were having a little too much fun at that dance class. Plus you always came home smelling like chlorine."

"Let me go!" Tank yelled as he struggled to wiggle free of his brother. "Let me go, you big ape!"

"Knock it off. I'm not going to let you go. Not until we have a little talk." Zack pinned Tank against the wall.

"You little worms think you're so smart trading places, don't you?" Zack said. "What are Mom and Dennis going to say when they find out?"

"They're not going to find out," Tank cried.

"Sure they will," Zack said, twisting Tank's arm behind his back.

"Ow!"

"You know I can't keep a secret like this."

"You'd better!" Tank yelled, thrashing around.

Jason winced. He wished Tank would shut up. Didn't he realize he was making things worse?

Zack pulled Tank to the floor and plopped down on his stomach.

"Oof!" Tank cried. It looked like all the air had gone out of him.

"Hey, you're hurting him," Jason said, stepping forward.

Zack turned and narrowed his eyes at Jason. "Who asked you?"

Jason took three steps back. He felt like the Cowardly Lion in the Wizard of Oz. But he wasn't any match for someone Zack's size.

Zack turned back to Tank. "Now," he said nicely. "You want me to keep my mouth shut around Mom and Dennis. What's it worth to you?"

"Er arph ee."

"What?"

"*Er arph ee!*" Tank repeated, shoving Zack.

"He said, 'Get off me,' " Jason said in a small voice. At least, that was what he *thought* Tank said.

"Get off you?" Zack asked Tank. "You want me to get off you?" He laughed. "Well, that's going to cost you extra."

Zack rolled off Tank. Tank slowly raised himself to a sitting position and rubbed his stomach.

Zack turned to Jason. "How much have you got?"

"Me?" Jason blinked.

"Yes, you," Zack said impatiently. "You're in this too, aren't you? What have you got on you?"

"I-I-I'm not s-sure," Jason said. He scuttled across the room to his backpack and with shaky fingers opened the front pocket. "I-I've got about three dollars in change," he said. "Is that enough?"

Zack snatched the change out of Jason's hand. "It's a start. What about you, Thomas-the-Tank?" Zack grabbed one of Tank's tennis shoes and reached inside. "How much have you got stashed in here today?" He pulled his fist out and opened it. "Five bucks? Not too shabby."

"You're not really going to tell on us, are you?" Jason asked.

"I don't know," Zack replied, blowing his hair out of his eyes. "I just can't make up my mind."

"I've got another five bucks hidden in my sock drawer," Tank said grudgingly. "You can have it if you keep your mouth shut."

Zack scratched his head. "Well, I could *maybe* keep

my mouth shut. But then again, maybe I couldn't." He looked pointedly at Jason.

"I-I-I could probably bring five dollars to school tomorrow and give it to Tank," Jason said.

Zack looked at the money in his hand. "So that's five, ten, fifteen, sixteen, seventeen, eighteen dollars and twelve cents."

"Hmm..." he said, tapping his foot. "Yeah, that's probably enough to keep me quiet. It'll at least buy me that new Bad Dogs CD I've been wanting. Thanks a lot, guys." He stood up and ruffled Tank's hair. "Always a pleasure doing business with you."

And then he was gone.

Jason and Tank finished up in silence.

Jason wet his hair down.

And Tank dried his under the hand drier.

Jason felt like he should say something, but before he could even clear his throat, Tank said, "Shut up, Dork Face."

* * *

"Jason's swimming test is a week from Thursday," Dagmar announced at dinner a few nights later. "I assume we're all going to go?"

Jason's fork clattered to the floor.

"That's right!" Mom said. "You haven't let us watch any of your lessons, but we'll definitely be there to see you pass your test."

Jason picked up his fork. "Uh, you don't have to," he said. "I mean, I know how busy you all are."

"But we've all been waiting so long to see you pass," Dagmar said sweetly.

Jason stared at his sister. Since when did she care about his swimming test?

"I think I can get the afternoon off," Dad said.

"We *all* want to see you take your test," Dagmar said.

"No, really," Jason argued. "Having you guys there will make me too nervous."

"But Ms. Hall says you've been doing so well. Why would you be nervous?" Mom asked.

"Yeah, Jason." Dagmar leered at him. "Are you afraid you suddenly won't be able to put your face in the water?"

Jason gasped. Did she know?

No, she couldn't. The only people who knew were he and Tank and all those girls in the dance class. And now Zack.

"No," he said finally. "I just want to do this by myself."

"I'm sorry, Jason," Mom said. "But I have to see you pass your test. It's too big a milestone for me to miss."

"Make sure you bring the video camera, too," Dagmar said, smiling sweetly at Jason.

Jason groaned. He and Tank could fool their

teachers and most of the students in their classes, but there was no way they could fool Jason's parents. No way at all.

What were they going to do?

After dinner, Dagmar stopped Jason in the hallway. "Does the name Zack Talbott mean anything to you?" she asked.

Jason's stomach dropped. "You know him?"

"He's in my science class," Dagmar said, leaning against the wall and smiling. "I think he's kind of cute. Don't you?"

Jason snorted. "I love his earring," he muttered as he went into his room.

Dagmar followed. "He's really observant. He's probably the most observant person I've ever met. No one can fool him."

"Yeah, well...if you like him so much, why don't you get him to ask you out on a date?" Jason asked. "I happen to know he's got plenty of money!"

Dagmar laughed. "Yeah, I heard about that."

So she *did* know. "I suppose you're going to tell Mom and Dad?"

"No." Dagmar shook her head. "I think that should be your job." She started to go across the hall to her room, then turned back. "You do realize, don't you, Jason, that one way or another you're going to have to learn to swim?"

91

"Butt out!" Jason slammed his door. He started pacing back and forth. He and Tank had problems. Big problems.

Just when he thought things couldn't possibly get any worse, the telephone rang. "Jason, it's for you!" Dad called. Jason went to the phone.

It was Tank.

"You're not going to believe this," Tank said. "Mrs. Kaplan just called my mom and asked her to bring cupcakes to that end-of-class ball of yours."

"WHAT?" Jason cried.

"After my mom got done yelling at me for not telling her about this little wing-ding she said, 'No way am I missing that!' "

Jason told Tank about his family insisting on watching him take his swimming test.

Tank sighed heavily. "We are in deep doo-doo, Dork Face."

16
Trading Places Again

T here's no other way," Tank said finally. "You'll have to teach me how to dance and I'll have to teach you how to swim."

Jason switched the receiver to his other hand. "Oh sure."

"Come on. It can't be that hard. We'll work every day after school and all weekend. And then we'll just switch back on that last day. No problem."

No problem? After everything that had happened, Jason was right back where he'd started.

"I'll teach you how to dance, but you'll never be able to teach me how to swim."

Tank laughed. "Dork Face! If *I* can learn to dance, *you* can learn to swim."

Like dancing was the same as swimming.

"Just forget it," Jason said. He didn't have a prayer.

"No! Listen to me. Tomorrow, after school, you and me are going to the pool."

"No, we aren't."

"Yes, we are! And then I'm going over to your house with you afterwards and you're going to show me how to dance."

Jason didn't say anything.

"I'll meet you by the fence after school. You better be there. Or else!"

* * *

"Okay, the first thing you have to do is put your face in the water," Tank said as the two of them stood at one end of the shallow section of the pool. Jason had told his mom he was going swimming with a friend. Like now that he could swim, he was going to be hanging out at the pool all the time. Just like Dagmar.

Right.

Jason shivered. "I already told you. I can't."

"Sure you can. It's easy. Watch." Tank took a deep breath, then plunged his whole body under the water.

Jason stepped back to avoid getting splashed.

Tank surfaced and shook the water out of his hair. He didn't even rub his eyes. "Now you do it."

Jason shook his head.

Tank sighed. "Why not?"

"I don't like getting water up my nose."

"So plug your nose," Tank said.

Jason took a deep breath, plugged his nose and quickly popped his face in and out of the water.

"There. Now was that so bad?" Tank asked.

Jason rubbed his eyes. "I can't swim one-handed."

For the next hour, Tank tried to coax Jason into putting his face in the water without plugging his nose. No luck.

"This is hopeless," Jason said as they sat outside the Rec Center and waited for his mom.

"No, it's not," Tank argued. "We'll work on it more tomorrow. You're going to learn to swim, Dork Face. You're going to learn to swim if it kills me!"

It's going to kill me, not you, Jason thought.

When Jason's mother picked them up, Dagmar was sitting in the front seat.

"How was your swim?" Mom asked.

"Great!" Jason plastered a fake smile to his face. *No problem.*

"So, Tank." Dagmar turned to rest her chin against the back of her seat. "Tell me about Zack. What does he like to do in his spare time?"

Tank shrugged. "I don't know."

"Does he play any sports?"

"No."

"Me, neither. I mean, I used to swim, but I don't anymore," she said. As though anybody cared. "Does he like to read or play computer games?"

"Not really," Tank replied.

Dagmar seemed to be racking her brain trying to figure out what else Zack might be into.

"He's in a band," Tank offered.

"He is?" Dagmar's eyes widened. "I've thought about joining a band."

Mom glanced away from the road just long enough to raise an eyebrow at Dagmar.

"I have," Dagmar insisted. "I can sing."

Jason snorted. "You can not!"

"I can too!" She glared at Jason, then fixed her eyes on Tank. "Do you know if he needs a female lead for his band? Will you ask him for me?"

"Ask him yourself," Tank replied.

Dagmar twirled her hair thoughtfully. "Maybe I will." Finally she turned around.

Tank leaned over and whispered in Jason's ear. "Does she have a thing for my brother or what?"

"Maybe," Jason whispered back.

"She's crazy," Tank whispered.

But the way Jason saw it, if Dagmar and Zack got together, old Zack would be the crazy one.

After dinner, Jason and Tank locked themselves into Jason's room. Jason turned on his radio and tuned to the heavy metal station so no one would guess what they were doing. Then he tried to teach Tank the simple box step.

Forward-side-together. Back-side-together.

"Not like that!" Jason said.

"What?" Tank stomped his foot. "I'm doing exactly what you're doing!"

"Yeah, but you're not doing it the way I'm doing it. Look, this is what you're doing." Jason made like he was an elephant and stomped around.

"You making fun of me, Dork Face?" Tank asked, jabbing his finger into Jason's chest. "Because I could've made fun of you earlier at the pool. But I didn't."

"I'm not making fun of you," Jason said. "I'm just showing you what you look like."

"Yeah, well, here's what *you* looked like in the pool." Tank scrunched his eyes and nose up and made a face like he'd just bit into a lemon. Then he made a big show of plugging his nose and bringing his face down into an imaginary pool of water.

Jason ignored that. "Do you want to learn how to dance or not?" he asked, crossing his arms.

Tank looked at Jason warily. "I don't know," he said. "I don't know if I can."

"Sure, you can," Jason said. He showed Tank the steps again. "You know the moves, you just have to do them gracefully."

Tank tried again. He still looked like an elephant with two left feet.

"Feel the rhythm," Jason said.

"Oh, I feel the rhythm, all right," Tank said. He wiggled his neck to the heavy metal music.

Jason flopped on his bed and tuned his radio to

the love song station. "Maybe this will help."

Forward-side-together. Back-side-together.

"That's a little better," Jason said, his eyes glued to Tank's feet.

Tank grinned. He kept at it.

By the end of the night, Tank's box step was almost as graceful as Jason's. "This isn't so bad," Tank admitted. "But don't tell anyone I said so."

"No one's going to know you didn't go to all the dance lessons," Jason said.

"Thanks," Tank said shyly. "And don't worry. We'll have you swimming by next Thursday, too."

"Sure," Jason said, forcing a smile. But deep down he knew there was no way he'd be swimming by next Thursday.

No way at all.

* * *

"I've got an idea," Tank said the next day. He and Jason were getting changed into their swimming trunks.

"You do? What?"

Tank held up a pair of nose plugs.

"*Nose plugs?*" Jason cried. "What good are those?"

"They'll keep the water out of your nose." He tossed them to Jason. "Put them on."

"I don't know," Jason said. "They look kind of uncomfortable."

"Of course they're uncomfortable," Tank said. "What do you expect? They pinch your nose shut. They'll keep the water out, though. I promise."

As tight as they were, Jason didn't doubt that for a minute. "But what's the point? You don't wear nose plugs, so I can't exactly show up wearing them. Even if I could, they probably wouldn't let me use them for a test."

"Hmm." Tank scratched his ear. "Good point. Well, even if you can't wear them for the test, you can still wear them now. Maybe I can teach you how to do the crawl stroke with them on? Then we'll work on putting your face in the water without them later."

"Okay," Jason said. It couldn't hurt to try.

He pried the nose plugs open as wide as he could go, then put them on. "They're too tight," he complained. "I can't breathe! I can't breathe at all!" It was just like last summer when he fell out of Grandpa's boat and water poured into his mouth and nose.

"Chill out," Tank said. "Just breathe through your mouth." Like this. Tank took a deep breath in, then let it out. In and out. In and out.

Jason tried to match Tank's rhythm. It was okay. He was breathing. He was just breathing through his mouth rather than his nose.

"Come on." Tank led Jason out to the pool.

Tank jumped right in, but Jason sat down at the

edge of the pool and readjusted his nose plugs. They really hurt his nose.

"Would you just get in the pool!" Tank cried.

Jason slowly lowered his body into the water.

There weren't many people here yet for a Sunday afternoon. A couple of people were swimming laps in the middle section. Jason and Tank had most of the pool to themselves.

"Okay. All you have to do is take a deep breath, close your mouth, and put your face in the water. You should be able to do it with nose plugs on."

"I'll try," Jason said. He took a deep breath and quickly touched his chin to the water. Then he closed his eyes and put his whole face in. He counted to five and then raised his head. Water dripped from his chin. *He did it!*

"That wasn't bad," Tank said as Jason rubbed his eyes.

Jason practiced putting his face in the water a few more times. Then Tank said, "Why don't you let me show you how to do the crawl stroke. First we'll do it out of the water."

"Okay," Jason said, hoisting himself out of the pool.

Tank showed Jason how to move his arms and when to turn his head. There was a definite rhythm to the whole thing. Kind of like dancing. Except instead of forward-side-together, back-side-together, the rhythm was reach and pull, turn and breathe. Which was a lot more complicated.

When Jason tried it with his face in the water, he never had his arm in the right place when he was ready to turn his head and breathe.

"Keep trying," Tank said. "You'll get it."

Jason put his face in the water and tried again. He reached and pulled, turned and breathed. Once. Then he stopped to brush the water off his face.

"That was okay," Tank said. "But quit wiping your face. A little water isn't going to kill you."

They kept at it until Jason could do a few strokes without stopping to wipe his face.

"Way to go, Dork Face!" Tank cheered when Jason finally did it. "Now why don't you see if you can go from here all the way to the wall?"

Jason glanced down the length of the pool. He and Tank were standing in the middle of the shallow section. As long as he had his nose plugs, he could maybe do it. "Okay," he said. "I'll try."

Jason adjusted his nose plugs and started swimming. Reach and pull. Turn and breathe. Reach and pull. Turn and breathe.

How far was he? he wondered. Halfway there? Three-quarters of the way there? He couldn't open his eyes in the water, so he had no idea.

Rather than risk ramming head-first into the wall, Jason stopped reaching and pulling and turning and breathing. He held his arms out in front of him and waited for his fingers to touch the wall. He hoped he had enough air to make it.

Yes, he did! His hands banged against the wall and he stood up and rubbed his eyes and face. "Ha! I did it!" he shrieked. He opened his eyes and saw Tank was right beside him.

"Okay. Now, take off the nose plugs," Tank said.

Jason slapped his hand over his nose. "No way," he cried, leaping away from Tank.

Tank followed him. "After going so long with nose plugs, your nose already knows not to breathe in the water. So take them off and try it!"

"No!"

Tank sighed. "Well, we've still got a few more days," he said. "You'll be able to take the nose plugs off by then."

"Don't bet on it," Jason said.

* * *

"Luke called," Jason's mom said when he got home. Jason slapped his hand to his head. He had never called Luke back.

Jason reached for the cordless phone and punched in Luke's new phone number.

Luke's mom answered the phone. "I'll go get him for you, Jason," she said.

Jason took the phone up to his room, where he could talk in private.

"Jason?" Luke said in a distant voice. "Jason who? I don't know any Jason. Oh, wait a minute. Yeah. I had a friend named Jason. A long, long, time ago."

"Oh, come on," Jason said as he flopped down on his bed. "It hasn't been that long."

"You never called me back."

"I know. I'm sorry. I've just had a lot to do."

"Like what?"

Jason told Luke about him and Tank getting caught and how he had to teach Tank how to dance and Tank had to trying to teach him to swim—

"What, are you and Tank *friends* now?"

Jason blinked. *Were* he and Tank friends? They'd been spending a lot of time hanging out. And not just to practice dancing and swimming. They'd been eating lunch together. Working on Jason's script together.

"I-I don't know," Jason said. He couldn't be friends with Tank Talbott. Tank was the kid who had made Luke's life miserable. And yet...

"I think Tank's different than he used to be," Jason tried to explain.

Luke snorted. "People like Tank don't change."

"Sure they do," Jason said.

"Hmm. Maybe. You've sure changed," Luke said quietly.

"What do you mean?" He was still the same old Jason. Wasn't he? Even though he had forgotten to call Luke back.

"I don't know," Luke said. "We've both got other friends now and that's okay. I just wish Tank Talbott wasn't one of your friends."

"I'm not sure he is," Jason said.

"Well, it sure sounds like he is to me."

17
All Figured Out?

O kay!" Kelly plopped her tray down next to Jason's during lunch on Tuesday. "I think I figured it out!"

"Hey!" Tank cried from across the table. "What do you think you're doing?"

"It's a free country. I can sit here if I want to. Besides, I'm a friend of Jason's." Kelly smiled at Jason as she opened her milk.

"That's Kelly. From dance class," Jason explained. In other words, she wasn't his friend and he wasn't any happier about her joining them than Tank was.

"Let me tell you what I figured out," Kelly said.

Jason and Tank exchanged a glance. It didn't look like they could stop her.

"First of all, Tank Talbott is not the kind of guy to sign up for Ballroom Dancing for Kids."

"You got that right!" Tank said.

"So I bet his mom is making him go. She probably thought it would turn him into a nicer person or something."

Tank raised an eyebrow at Kelly, but he didn't say anything.

"I also don't think Tank Talbott is the kind of guy who pays people to do stuff for him. He's the kind of guy who makes people pay him. Like if they don't want to get beaten up or something."

"Tank's not like that," Jason said quickly. Not lately, at least.

"How do you know I'm not?" Tank glared at Jason.

What? Was that what Tank wanted people to think?

"Either way." Kelly clearly did not like being interrupted. "I don't think Tank's paying you to go to his dance class, Jason. I think you go because you want to."

Jason listened nervously as Kelly went on. Did she really have it all figured out?

"You're not like other boys, Jason," Kelly said, lowering her voice. "You're much nicer. And since you're nicer, I bet you like to dance."

Jason did like to dance. Sort of.

"I saw a movie about a kid who wanted to be a professional dancer," Kelly said. "But his parents wouldn't let him. He had to sneak his lessons. And I bet that's what you're doing. I bet you're sneaking dance classes wherever and whenever you can, by trading places with boys who are signed up for dance, but don't want to be there!"

Jason just about choked. That wasn't right! That wasn't right at all!

"Yup! That's it!" Tank said, a big grin spreading across his face. "You got it!"

"TANK!" Jason cried.

"Come on, Dork Face." Tank cocked his head. "There's no use pretending anymore. She figured it out! And it's okay. I can tell she doesn't think any less of you."

"Oh, no!" Kelly shook her head. "Not at all. In fact, that was why I came over here." Kelly patted Jason's arm. "I don't think there's anything wrong with boys wanting to dance. I think it's nice."

Jason yanked his arm out of Kelly's reach.

"Maybe one day your parents will understand and sign you up for classes legally," Kelly said.

"We can hope." Tank nodded with sympathy.

Jason almost kicked Tank under the table.

"Well..." Kelly stood up. "You guys have been interesting subjects."

Jason was almost afraid to ask. "Interesting subjects?"

"Yes. There are always reasons why people do the things they do. A psychologist's job is to figure out those reason. I'm not a psychologist yet, but I'm going to be one someday." She smiled. "Ta ta," she said, with a little wave. And then she was gone.

Jason dropped his head to his hands. "Why did you let her think all that stuff about me wanting to be a dancer?"

Tank smiled. "Would you rather she find out that you can't swim?"

"I don't know," Jason said. It was hard to decide which one would be worse.

"Trust me. It's better this way," Tank said. "She thinks she's got us all figured out, so that means she'll probably quit bugging us."

Okay, Jason thought. One problem down, one *bigger* problem to go.

* * *

On Wednesday, Jason and Tank went to the pool one last time before Jason's swimming test. They sat down together at the edge of the shallow section.

"You really don't need these nose plugs, Dork Face." Tank held the plugs out of Jason's reach.

"I need the nose plugs, Tank."

"No, you don't."

"Yes, I do!"

Tank sighed. "Okay, but just for a little bit." He tossed the nose plugs at Jason. "Then you have to give them back and try it on your own, okay? I mean it this time!"

"Okay." Jason put the nose plugs on and swam the entire length of the pool. Twice.

"Good!" Tank clapped when Jason touched the wall. He held out his hand. "Now give me the nose plugs."

"No!" Jason turned away.

"GIVE THEM TO ME, DORK FACE!"

"NO!" He'd never stood up to Tank like this before. He half expected Tank to jump into the water, yank the plugs off Jason's head, and shove his face in the water.

But he didn't.

"Come on, Jason," Tank pleaded. "Please? The test is tomorrow. What are you going to do if you can't swim without your nose plugs?"

Tank had called him Jason instead of Dork Face? Tank had said *please?*

"I don't know," Jason said. About the only thing he could do was pray for a miracle.

* * *

Jason woke up on Thursday morning knowing he was in serious trouble. His whole family was coming to watch him take the test.

Jason took Tank's nose plugs to school. He took them out during recess. "There has to be a way I can use these nose plugs today," he said. "There has to be a reason why I'd need them."

"I can't think of one." Tank aimed the ball at the basket and missed.

Jason caught the ball on the rebound and tossed it back to Tank. "What about a sinus infection? If someone had a sinus infection, wouldn't they wear nose plugs if they wanted to go swimming?"

"Maybe," Tank said as he aimed for the basket again. This time he sunk it. He smiled. "Or..." he said, looking at Jason with a mysterious gleam in his eye.

"Or what?"

"Meet me in the downstairs bathroom after school," Tank said. "I think I've got an idea."

* * *

Tank peered under all the toilet stalls in the bathroom.

"What are you doing?" Jason asked.

"Making sure we're alone," Tank responded. He opened his backpack and took out a pair of scissors and a Band-Aid.

"Give me the nose plugs." Tank held out his hand.

"What for?" Jason asked uneasily.

"Just give me the nose plugs!"

Jason dug the nose plugs out of his pocket and handed them to Tank. He watched in horror as Tank snipped off the cord on both sides.

"What'd you do that for?" Jason asked.

Tank didn't answer. He gave the plugs to Jason. "Put them on."

Jason did.

Then Tank pulled the Band-Aid out of its wrapper, tore the papers off the sticky parts and stuck the Band-Aid over Jason's nose plugs. "Here. You can tell people I beat you up or something. That's why you've got this Band-Aid on your nose."

Jason glanced at himself in the mirror. You could hardly even see the bumps from the plugs. He grinned. "Hey, that's a good idea!" He sounded all stuffed up when he talked. "But—" he looked at Tank. "I'm not going to tell people you beat me up."

"Why not?" Tank shrugged. "It's the kind of thing I'd do, isn't it?"

Was he joking?

"No, it's not." Jason shook his head.

Tank snorted. "I don't think your buddy Luke would agree with you."

Jason wasn't about to let that go by. "Yeah, well, maybe I know you better than Luke. Luke never really got to know you."

"That's true." Tank leaned against a sink and picked at his fingernail. "You know, I threw a walnut at his head the day I moved in next door to him. I was just sort of joking. And he ran crying to his mom and I felt stupid. That's how it was the whole time. I'd do something to him and he went crying to the nearest grown-up." Tank looked at Jason. "I wish it hadn't been like that."

"So does he," Jason said.

"No. I mean I wish I hadn't done that stuff. Who knows? Maybe we could've been friends."

Jason rubbed his Band-Aid nervously.

"A-are you and I friends, Tank?"

Tank looked down at his dirty tennis shoes. "I don't know. Are we?"

"I don't know. I guess so."

"Yeah. I guess so," Tank agreed. He let out a big breath of air and moved away from the sink. He looked at Jason's Band-Aid. "Let's say you got hit in the nose with a basketball."

Jason grinned. "That's something I would do." He checked in the mirror. The Band-Aid seemed secure. Hopefully it would stay on in the water.

"Yeah, it is," said Tank. But he was grinning, too. "Hey, good luck today," he said.

"Thanks," said Jason. "You, too."

* * *

"Jason! What happened to your nose?" Mom rolled down her window as the car pulled up in front of him after school.

Jason opened the back door and got in beside his

sister. His dad was sitting in front next to his mom.

Jason swallowed hard, which made his ears pop because of the nose plugs. "I uh, hurt it. In gym."

Dagmar looked at him skeptically. Like she knew something wasn't right with his story, but she didn't know what.

"Are you all right?" Mom asked with concern.

"Oh, yeah. The nurse said I'm fine," Jason said with a dismissive wave of his hand."

He breathed in and out through his mouth. He wouldn't be able to breathe through his nose again until after the swimming test.

Dagmar squinted at him some more. Could she see the bumps of the nose plugs underneath the Band-Aid?

"Maybe you should take your Band-Aid off so Mom and Dad can see your nose," Dagmar said. "See if you need stitches or something."

"Oh no. That's not necessary," Jason said, turning away so she wouldn't have such a good view of his nose. "Besides, I'd hate to be late to my swimming test!" In and out, he breathed through his mouth. In and out.

"As long as your school nurse looked at it, I'm sure it's fine," Dad said.

Mom put the car in gear and pulled away from the curb.

Jason leaned back against his seat and sighed. All he had to do was get through the next hour. Then he could breathe through his nose again. He'd have his certificate from tadpole swimming. And his life would return to normal.

18
Another Test

There weren't many kids in the Rec Center changing room when Jason arrived. He went to the far corner of the bench to get changed. He was scared. Scared that people would think he wasn't really "Jason." Which was sort of funny when you thought about it. Imagine somebody not thinking you're the person that you are!

He touched the Band-Aid on his nose to make sure it was still in place. It was. His nose hurt, but there was nothing he could do about it. As soon as the test was over, he could come back in here, take the nose plugs out and put the Band-Aid back on. He'd probably have to wear the Band-Aid for a few days, but he could live with that.

Jason pulled on his swimming trunks and wondered how Tank was doing. Was he nervous, too? Would he remember to move his feet gracefully?

As soon as he got out to the pool area, Ms. Hall called, "Jason! What happened to your nose?"

Jason stopped. One thing about this Band-Aid trick, it called *more* attention to him.

"I hurt it in gym," he said in a nasally voice.

"Oh, that's too bad," Ms. Hall replied. She looked concerned. But at least she didn't come over to get a closer look.

He glanced over at the bleachers at the other end of the pool. His parents and sister had front row seats. Mom and Dad waved. Dagmar rested her feet on the railing and pretended she wasn't with them.

Jason checked his Band-Aid again. Still secure.

Ms. Hall blew on her whistle and raised her hand to get everyone's attention. "Listen up, tadpoles," she said. "Today is your swimming test."

Cheers rang out from all around the pool.

Jason swallowed hard. This was it. The moment of truth.

"There are three parts to the test," Ms. Hall explained for all the kids who hadn't already been through tadpole swimming three times. "Back float for two minutes. Tread water for two minutes. And the crawl stroke. I'll time your back floats. Ms. Wyatt will watch you tread water." A woman whose brown hair was piled on her head waved to everyone from the middle section of the pool. "And Mr. Abram will be observing your crawl strokes," Ms. Hall said.

Mr. Abram!

Why did Mr. Abram have to be there? And why did he have to be in charge of the crawl stroke?

"It doesn't matter which station you go to first,"

Ms. Hall said. "Just make sure you get to all three. Okay, everyone in the pool!"

"All right!"

"Hooray!"

Kids shrieked as they dive-bombed into the pool.

Jason trembled. He couldn't go over there and do the crawl stroke for Mr. Abram. No way would Mr. Abram believe he had gotten over his fear of putting his face in the water.

On the other hand, seeing *is* believing. Both in the movies and in real life.

Jason touched the Band-Aid on his nose. As long as he was wearing nose plugs, he *could* put his face in the water.

He glanced over at his family.

"Good luck!" Mom mouthed at him.

Dad gave him a thumbs up.

Dagmar's arms were folded. She just stared at him.

Jason raised his eyes to the ceiling. *Let me pass*, he thought. *Please let me pass!*

"What are you doing?" a little kid with blue trunks asked, wrinkling his nose. The kid looked up at the ceiling, then looked back at Jason.

"Uh, nothing. I'm just trying to decide where to start."

The kid shrugged, then dive-bombed into the pool.

Jason decided to start with the easiest part of the test. The back float. He walked around to the middle section of the pool and lowered himself into the water. Three other kids were already there. "Are you guys ready?" Ms. Hall asked.

"Yes!" Jason said in unison with the other kids.

"Okay, when I say go, lie back. I'll let you know when your time is up." Ms. Hall stared at her watch. "Go!"

Jason lay back. But while he was lying there he worried about his nose sticking up for everyone to see. Was the Band-Aid still on straight? Did it cover the lumpy nose plugs?

"That's two minutes," Ms. Hall said almost right away.

"Hooray, Jason!" his parents cheered from the bleachers.

Jason went to tread water next. This was the second easiest part of the test. It was like riding a bike in the water.

While Jason moved his arms and legs, he watched the kids who were doing the crawl stroke from one end of the shallow section to the other. Those kids made it look so easy.

"Pass," Ms. Wyatt said after two minutes.

"Hooray, Jason!" his parents cheered again.

Now, the only thing standing in the way of his freedom was the dreaded crawl stroke. Jason walked over to the other side of the pool. He checked his Band-Aid. It was a little wet now, but it was still in place.

"So, Jason Pfeiffer." Mr. Abram grinned. "Here we are again."

Could Mr. Abram see Jason's nose plugs through his Band-Aid? If anyone could, Mr. Abram could.

"Why don't you get in the water and let's see what you can do," Mr. Abram said.

Jason sat down at the edge of the pool the way he normally did to get in the water. But on second thought, he stood up, took a deep breath, closed his eyes and mouth, and cannonballed into the pool. *Wow! That was sort of fun!* Jason thought as he stood up. Water dripped from his face.

But if Mr. Abram was impressed, he didn't show it. "You know the drill. All the way across. Head in the water. Begin whenever you're ready."

Jason was as ready as he'd ever be. He closed his eyes, put his face in the water, and kicked off. He paddled his arms just like Tank had shown him, taking a breath whenever he needed one.

So far so good.

Since he still couldn't open his eyes in the water, he had no idea how much farther he had to go. *Don't worry about it*, he told himself. *Just keep going.*

The nose plugs kept the water out of his nose. All

Jason had to do was paddle his arms and kick his feet and turn his head to breathe.

He had to be close to the edge now. Had to be!

Finally, his fingers hit concrete. He stood up and rubbed the water out of his eyes. He'd done it! He'd really done it!

He looked up and saw his parents and sister standing right above him.

"Way to go, Jason!" Dad said.

"We're so proud of you!" Mom said.

"Thanks," Jason said, reaching up to scratch his nose. As he did, his Band-Aid rubbed off in his hand.

19
Coming Clean

Whats that thing on your nose?" Dad peered curiously at Jason. Jason yanked the nose plugs off and massaged his sore nose.

"Nose plugs?" Dagmar shrieked.

"I thought you said you hurt your nose in gym class," Mom said.

"Well, I—" How was he supposed to explain this?

By now the lifeguards, teachers, and other students had gathered around.

"Hey Jason!" one of the kids laughed. "Why were you wearing a Band-Aid and nose plugs?"

Jason shivered. He lowered his body into the water until only his head remained above the surface.

"Because he can't put his face in the water!" Dagmar spoke for him.

"BUTT OUT!" Jason yelled at her.

"Jason can put his face in the water," Ms. Hall said, her forehead wrinkling in confusion. "He's been doing it all session."

Dagmar shook her head. "No, he hasn't," she said. "Tank Talbott has been doing it for him! Tank Talbott has been taking Jason's swimming lessons."

"Tank Talbott?" Mom looked at Jason. "You mean that new friend of yours?"

Before Jason could answer, Dagmar said, "And guess what Jason's been doing for Tank?"

"WOULD YOU JUST SHUT UP?" Jason exploded.

"Jason!" Mom said sharply.

"What?" Jason stomped his foot on the pool floor. "I'm tired of her butting in on everything. I don't want her telling it."

"Then you tell it," Dad said.

"Okay. Fine." Jason hoisted himself out of the water and sat there at the edge of the pool, dripping wet. Mom laid a towel around his shoulders.

Everyone was waiting.

Jason took a deep breath, then began. "It's true, all right? Tank *has* been taking my swimming lessons. And I've...I've been taking his dance lessons. It seemed like a good idea at first. He didn't want to learn to dance. And I couldn't learn to swim. So we traded places. But then everything got complicated. I had to quickly teach Tank how to dance and he had to try and teach me how to swim. Except the only way I could do it was with nose plugs. And I couldn't show up with nose plugs on the last day of the class. So that's why I had a Band-Aid over my nose."

At first nobody said anything.

Ms. Hall was the one to break the silence. "So

you're telling me that wasn't you who worked so hard that day to put your face in the water? That was some other kid putting on a big show?"

Jason gulped. "Sort of," he said in a small voice. Was Tank going to be in trouble now, too?

"Now I know why you were such a good dancer that day in your room," Mom said.

Jason couldn't even look at his mom.

"I don't know how these boys could've gotten away with this," Ms. Hall said. "How could I not have known this was a different kid in my class?"

"You only saw him once," Mr. Abram said. "This isn't the kind of thing you expect a kid to do."

"I'm sorry I lied," Jason said. He looked up at his parents. "But I keep telling you I'm not Dagmar! I can't swim! You can make me take lessons from now until forever and I'll never be able to do it."

"But you *can* do it," Ms. Hall said.

"No, I can't." That was why he and Tank had traded places.

"Sure, you can. That was you out there today, wasn't it? Not this other boy."

Jason glanced up at Ms. Hall. "Well, yeah."

"So, you can float on your back. You can tread water. And you can swim one length of the pool with your face in the water." Ms. Hall smiled. "If that's not swimming, I don't know what is."

"But I wore nose plugs," Jason said.

"Sometimes Olympic swimmers use nose plugs," one of the lifeguards said. "It's no big deal."

No big deal? Really?

"You mean I could've walked in here with nose plugs and still passed?" Jason squeaked. "*D-did* I pass?" He held his breath.

Ms. Hall and Mr. Abram exchanged a look.

"I guess so," Ms. Hall replied.

"Even though he skipped most of the classes?" Mom asked.

"He did everything on the test," Mr. Abram said. "So he met all the requirements of tadpole swimming."

"Yes!" Jason punched his fist in the air. No more swimming! He was finally free!

* * *

"So, that's it?" Dagmar said when they got home. She followed Mom and Dad to the kitchen table, where they stood sorting the mail. "You're really going to let him quit swimming lessons?"

"Yup," Jason said with a big grin. "They're really going to let me quit." He plopped his swimming bag down on a kitchen chair and headed for the fridge. He was starving.

"But you still can't swim," Dagmar said.

Jason helped himself to a handful of cheese squares

from the fridge and stuffed two into his mouth. "I can, too!" he said, insulted. Ms. Hall even said he could.

"I can back float. I can tread water. And I can swim one length of the pool!"

"With nose plugs!" Dagmar said.

"So?"

"So, you don't wear nose plugs in real life. You weren't wearing nose plugs on Grandpa's boat last summer."

Jason's stomach lurched. Why did she have to go and bring that up?

"What would happen if you fell in the water again this summer?" Dagmar asked. "Without your nose plugs?"

Jason popped another cheese square into his mouth. That was a stupid question.

"That's a good question." Dad set the mail down and looked at Jason. "Do you think you'd be able to save yourself?"

Jason stopped chewing. "I-I don't know." That panicky can't-breathe feeling was coming back.

"I bet you couldn't," Dagmar said.

"Who asked you?"

"I don't know," Mom said, glancing at Dad. "Maybe we should think about signing Jason up for a few more lessons?"

"Maybe we should," Dad agreed.

"WHAT?" Jason cried. "But that's not fair! We had a deal!"

"Jason—" Mom began.

"You said if I passed tadpole swimming, I wouldn't have to take more lessons. And I passed! You can't go back on that now!"

"If that's what we said, I think we made a mistake," Dad said. "This isn't about passing tadpole swimming. It's about learning to swim."

"That's right," Mom said. "We don't want what happened last summer to ever happen again."

"It won't!" That was the last thing Jason wanted, too. "I just won't go on Grandpa's boat again. If I stay away from water, I can't fall in."

"I'd rather you know what to do if you fall in than have you avoid the water completely," Mom said. "I'll call the Rec Center and see what the next class is after tadpole swimming."

Dad got the phone book out of the drawer and handed it to Mom. Mom flipped through pages with one hand while reaching for the phone with the other.

Jason couldn't believe this was happening.

"Thanks a lot!" He glared at Dagmar. This was all her fault. "What do you do? Stay awake nights thinking up new ways to torture me?"

"Torture you!" Dagmar looked shocked. "I'm not torturing you. I'm trying to save your life. Knowing how to swim could save your life."

"Yeah, right," Jason said. Like saving his life was important to Dagmar. He wasn't stupid. The only reason Dagmar wanted him to take more swimming lessons was because she knew how much he hated them.

"All you ever do is torture me," Jason said.

Dagmar put her hands on her hips. "For your information, I have not done one mean thing to you in like eight months!"

Jason laughed. That was such a lie!

"It's true. When was the last time I did anything to you?"

"Right now." As far as Jason was concerned, getting Mom and Dad to sign him up for more swimming lessons when they'd already promised he could quit was about the worst thing she'd ever done.

Dagmar let out a short laugh. "You never even noticed I quit picking on you. Probably because you're so busy picking on me."

"I pick on you?" Jason gaped at his sister. What a joke! She was bigger than him. Stronger than him. He'd have to have a death wish to take her on.

"You pick on me all the time," Dagmar said. She counted examples on her fingers. "You look at me and scream, you make fun of me, you call me names, you make me the subject of your horror movie..."

"Well—" That was baby stuff. She did a lot worse

to him. Jason had scars on his arms from places she'd scratched him with her Martian claws. She was always pushing him out of her way, twisting his arm behind his back, telling him to go play in traffic so she could be an only child again.

Though, now that Jason actually thought about it, he had to admit it had been a while since she'd done any of those things. Had it really been *eight months*?

Jason thought harder. She'd told everyone about him and Tank trading places today. She could've told right away when she first found out, but she didn't.

And there was the time she'd tossed his script into the garbage can, but she hadn't really hurt it any.

What else? There had to be other stuff she'd done to him. Times she'd hit him. Pushed him. Scratched him.

But Jason couldn't think of any.

Jason stared at his sister. It was possible she hadn't done much to him in eight months.

And he hadn't even noticed.

Just like the girls in Tank's dance class didn't notice that "Tank" had quit picking on them after the first class.

Jason blinked. "I don't get it," he said. "Why would you stop picking on me?"

"I don't know." Dagmar picked some fuzz off her shirt. "I just did."

"But why?" Like Kelly said, there had to be a reason. Everybody does stuff for a reason.

"The next guppy class is full," Mom said, hanging up the phone. "There isn't another class until summer."

"Couldn't you check someplace else?" Dagmar asked. "Maybe Jason could take lessons someplace else?"

"I think we can wait until the Rec Center has an opening," Mom said.

"But he's got to learn how to swim!" Dagmar said, her voice rising.

"He will."

"No, he's got to learn now!" Dagmar said, all panicky. "If you wait until summer, it might be too late!"

Too late? Too late for what?

"Hey, calm down, honey," Dad said.

But Dagmar was far from calm. Her eyes were practically on fire. Her fists were clenched. "You don't know what it was like last summer!" she cried. "You weren't there!"

Jason peered at his sister. Were those actual tears in her eyes? Oh, she was good. Pretending to cry just to get Mom and Dad to sign him up for more swimming lessons.

"Jason almost died! He almost died!"

Those *were* tears in Dagmar's eyes. And now those tears were streaming down her cheeks.

"Shh," Mom said, wrapping her arms around Dagmar. "It's okay."

"He almost died!"

"But he didn't."

"He could have." Dagmar pulled away from Mom. "I tried to help," she said, wiping the back of her hand across her cheeks. "But Grandpa yelled at me to stay by the boat."

"Grandpa was scared, honey," Mom said. "He was scared he wouldn't find Jason in time. And he didn't want to have to worry about you, too."

"But I can swim. I could've helped," Dagmar insisted. "I should have helped!"

"No, Dagmar." Dad shook his head. "You should've stayed in the boat. Just like Grandpa said."

Dagmar looked down at her feet. "But it was my fault he fell in," she said in a small voice.

"What?"

"It was." Dagmar sniffed. "I stood up when Grandpa caught that fish. And that made Jason lose his balance and fall in."

Was that what happened? Jason didn't remember. He didn't remember how he fell into the water. Just that he did.

"Dagmar." Dad grabbed Dagmar by the shoulders and looked into her eyes. "What happened to Jason was an accident. It wasn't your fault."

"That's right," Mom agreed. "There were several things that went wrong that day. For one thing, it was really windy. The water was choppy."

"And Jason wasn't wearing his life jacket like he should've been," Dad said.

"I had no idea this was still bothering you so much." Mom brushed the hair off Dagmar's forehead.

"We should've realized it," Dad said. "That must've been really scary to sit there by the boat, not knowing whether your brother would come up or not."

"It was." Dagmar nodded, sniffling.

Jason had never thought about what it must've been like for his sister sitting in the boat worrying about him.

"Did your decision to quit the swim team last fall have anything to do with what happened to Jason last summer?" Mom asked.

Dagmar wiped her cheeks again. "Sort of."

"Hey, I'm the one who almost drowned," Jason said. "Why would that make her want to quit her swim team?"

"Because every time I had practice, I had to see you at the other end of the pool. You couldn't do anything the teacher wanted you to do. You screamed every time they tried to get you to put your face in the water. It reminded me of what happened last summer."

Jason didn't quite know how to respond to that. He

had no idea his almost drowning had had such an effect on Dagmar. Was that why she'd quit picking on him, too? Because she felt so bad about what happened?

"You can't imagine what it's like to think someone's going to die right there in front of you," Dagmar said. "It's the worst thing in the world."

"But," Jason blinked.

"But what?" Dagmar asked.

"But you and I don't even like each other," Jason said. "So why would you care if I drowned?"

"Come on, Jason," Dad said in a serious tone of voice. "Think how you would feel if Dagmar were drowning. If you saw her go down and really thought she might not come back up again."

At first the idea didn't seem so bad. But once he really thought about it, really imagined his sister's head disappearing beneath the surface of the water, her lungs filling up with water, he felt like his own lungs were filling up with water. He couldn't breathe.

Dagmar was a pain in the butt. But she was still his sister. Drowning was just about the worst thing that could happen to a person.

Jason didn't want Dagmar to drown. Not really.

Maybe deep down, she actually felt the same way about him?

20
Another Beginning

I've got some bad news, Dork Face," Tank said on Friday afternoon. He and Jason were at the library. An assortment of film books, including the *Screen Writer's Market,* surrounded them.

"What is it?" Jason asked.

Tank unzipped his backpack, took out a sheet of paper and *The Dagmablob* script, and handed them to Jason.

"It's from Mortimer Caldwell!" Jason cried, his heart soaring. But his excitement soon fizzled. "He's rejecting us?"

Tank nodded. Jason read the letter.

Dear Mr. Talbott,
While your client's concept is an interesting one, I regret to inform you that I don't accept scripts from children. Please try me again in about five years.
Sincerely, Mortimer Caldwell.

"Look on the bright side," Tank said. "He told us to try again in five years. He must think we're at least thirteen now."

"Yeah, I guess," Jason said glumly. He plopped the script and letter down in the middle of the table. He had been so sure Mortimer Caldwell would snap up *The Dagmablob*. So sure he was on his way to movie stardom.

"Come on. Cheer up," Tank said, opening the *Screen Writer's Market*. "There are tons of other movie producers we can try. And one day, Mortimer Caldwell will be sorry he turned us down."

"Do you really think we should send *The Dagmablob* to anyone else?" Jason asked, flipping through the pages of his notebook. Maybe the script wasn't as good as he thought it was? In fact, what if it stunk and he didn't even know it?

"Are you kidding? Mortimer Caldwell is just one person. And you said yourself he's old. He's probably too old to know a good script when he sees one. But someone else will. I know it! Now come on. Let's make a list of all the people we can send it to."

"Okay," Jason said.

Tank handed him a sheet of paper and pencil and for the next few minutes they copied names and addresses.

Then Tank's head popped up. "Hey, you never told me about your swimming class. Did you pass?" He frowned. "You better have, after all that work I put in teaching you to swim."

Jason told Tank everything that had happened at the pool and later at home.

"Wow." Tank looked at Jason with new respect. "I didn't know you almost drowned last summer."

"Yeah."

"What's your next swimming class called?" Tank asked.

"Guppies."

"Guppies." Tank nodded. "Do you need me to take those classes for you?"

Jason grinned. "I think I can handle it. I can wear my nose plugs. And they said we'd work on going without the nose plugs."

"Good," Tank said. "Who knows? Maybe you'll learn to do without them."

"Maybe." He wasn't guaranteeing anything there. "What about you? How did your dance class go?"

Tank shrugged. "It was okay. Those girls were pretty out of control, though."

"What do you mean?"

"Well, it was weird. When my mom and I first walked into the gym, the girls all crowded around. At first I thought they were after my mom's cupcakes, but no. It was *me* they were after. 'Can I be your partner, Tank? Can I be your partner, Tank?'" he mimicked them.

Uh-oh. Jason had never warned the girls that he

and Tank were switching back for the last class. "So, what did you do?"

"I just said, 'Back off, women!' And they were like, 'Oh, no. It's really you, isn't it, Tank?' "

Jason could imagine the looks on the girls' faces. "Then what?"

"Then nothing. They left me alone. I danced with Mrs. Kaplan, ate some cupcakes and went home. End of story. I'll probably have to dance at my sister's wedding, but then I'll never have to dance again!"

"So, you didn't pick on any of those girls or anything?" Jason asked.

"Nah. I figured you probably hadn't been bugging them, so why should I?"

"What about Mrs. Kaplan?" Jason asked. "Did you really convince her that you were me? Or that I was you. Or, well, you know what I mean."

"She never suspected a thing. Neither did my mom. In fact, all Mrs. Kaplan did was talk about how much I've changed and how she's going to miss me." Tank got a thoughtful look on his face. "Nobody ever said that to me before, Dork Face. Usually people are glad to be rid of me."

"You're not a bad guy, Tank. If you'd just, well—" Jason didn't know how to put it.

"Act more like you?" Tank tried.

Another Beginning

That wasn't exactly what Jason meant. But... "Well, yeah, I guess," he said. "If you...did that...I think more people would like you."

Jason's heart pounded. Two months ago he probably would've gotten his face rearranged for suggesting Tank Talbott change the way he treated people.

But today Tank just nodded. "Maybe," he said. Maybe deep down Tank really did want people to like him?

"It's kind of weird how we fooled everyone, though, don't you think?" Tank asked. "You and I don't look that much alike."

Jason shrugged. "People see a guy with dark hair who answers to the name 'Tank,' they assume he's Tank. Or they see a guy with ducks on his swimsuit who answers to the name 'Jason,' they assume he's Jason."

"I guess," Tank said. "It's like once people get an idea in their heads, there's no changing their minds."

"But sometimes people do change," Tank said.
"Yeah. Sometimes they do," Jason agreed.

"Speaking of first impressions and whether they're right or wrong..." Tank picked up Jason's notebook. "I just got an idea. We should type up *The Dagmablob* on a computer before we send it out again. If it's typed no one will know it was written by a kid."

"Hey, that's a good idea," Jason said.

"How soon can you get that done?"

Jason shrugged. "I don't know. A week?"

"A week!" Tank cried. "It's going to take you a whole week to type that into a computer?"

"Well, if you can do it faster, why don't you do it?"

"Me?" Tank shook his head. "No way. Agents don't type."

"Why not?"

"They just don't."

"*There* you two are!" Dagmar called out. Jason looked up to find his sister and Tank's brother walking toward them. They were *holding hands*.

"Come on, you little worms," Zack said. "Let's hightail it out of here. Dagmar and I are going to a basketball game and Mom wants to drop you both off first."

Jason stared wide-eyed at them.

"What? You mean you two are going on a *date*?" Tank practically spit the word out.

Dagmar looked at Zack and smiled. Zack looked at Dagmar and smiled.

"Oh, brother!" Jason slapped his hand to his forehead. "What a nightmare."

"Can you imagine what would happen if they grow up, get married, and have kids?" Tank asked as he gathered up their things.

"Talk about scary." Jason shivered at the

possibility. Then he looked at Tank and grinned.

"What?" Tank glowered at him. "What are you grinning at now?"

Jason tilted his head toward Dagmar and Zack, who were busy making google eyes at each other. "I think I've got an idea for our next movie."

Tank glanced at them, then grinned at Jason. "Oh yeah?" he said as they followed Dagmar and Zack out of the library. "Let's hear it..."